She knew she'd been caught, but she wasn't worried. After all, she and Peter were much smarter than the cops…

Melissa knew someone had detected her, but they did nothing to stop the transfers. She knew she had left a footprint, but this was not the kind of detection system she normally saw when the police set up their own monitoring. They had to play by the rules or the evidence was useless, but this one was definitely thinking outside the box. She had seen something like this only during her MIT days and a classmate had written a tracer. She had used Peter's laptop to show him how easy it was to get the money and so they could never trace it to her unless of course they arrested Peter and he started crying. Even then, they wouldn't have evidence. Regardless, she would never transfer money out of Northwest again.

She knew what to do, even at MIT—she always used a public-access computer and someone else's account, whenever possible, without them knowing it. In a pinch, she got a fenced laptop, found public wireless access, took the money, and disposed of the computer—usually in a dumpster. She knew how not to leave an electronic footprint.

They never filed charges because they had no solid evidence, but she had been expelled.

To fight the expulsion, she might have given up evidence, so she walked away. It only returned to haunt her once when one employer actually called the registrar's office and asked. All MIT could say was she had been expelled. It could have been for any violation of the rules of conduct, something minor. She didn't get that job and it didn't matter. That was the other lesson she learned—be able to just walk away. Besides, there were more banks just as inept at security as Northwest.

Imagine dilettantes of Occupy Wall Street meeting and going head to head with the masters of the New World Order. One such rebel, Peter, turns on his rich banking family and takes up with a MIT computer-science drop out, Melissa. They plot to destroy the computer systems supporting the New York Stock Exchange. However, Peter's family takes a dim view of their activities and moves to intervene. Even if Peter and Melissa can outsmart the law—and cybercrimes private investigator Grady Marcs—they'll have a hard time escaping the wealthy globalists who will stop at nothing to keep their money safe and their dark secrets hidden.

In *Rogue Scion* by Shawn Rohrbach, Grady Marcs is a cybercrime private investigator, called in when a large bank discovers money missing from its depositors' accounts. Grady goes to work, uncovering a scheme to bring down the New World Order by a couple of rogue misfits, both from influential families. But these two don't just deal in computer theft, easily turning to murder to get what they want. As the bodies pile up, a chain of events is unleashed with far-reaching consequences that could ruin more than a few lives and bring down the world's economy. The story has a strong and complex plot that, despite the high tech cyber stuff, is still easy to follow. The author takes us into a world of crime and high finance, mingling high tech and conspiracy theories with good old-fashioned murder for an exciting read. ~ *Taylor Jones, Reviewer*

Rogue Scion by Shawn Rohrbach is a mystery/thriller combining new world order conspiracy theories, high tech computer crimes, and a mentally disturbed serial killer. Our protagonist, Grady Marcs, is a cybercrimes private investigator who is asked to investigate when a hacker robs a bank via a computer. Gone are the days when bank robbers wore masks and carried guns. All today's bank robbers need are a computer terminal, a mouse, and a whole lot of high tech knowledge. But while our hacker is good, Grady is better, and he uncovers far more than just a simple bank robbery. Positive that no one can track her, Melissa, the hacker, targets the NY Stock Exchange in an effort to stop a wealthy group of bankers, she calls the elite, from taking over the world. But Grady isn't the only one who can track her, and Peter, a son of one of those wealthy banking families soon shows up at her door. Rather than trying to stop her, Peter is a kindred spirit and he encourages her, even while knowing that her way will never work, as the elite are just too powerful. Peter has his own ideas on how to them bring down, and it doesn't involve hiding behind a computer. Whether or not you believe in a group of wealthy bankers trying to take over the world's economy, *Rogue Scion* hurls you into a world filled with misaligned loyalties, dark secrets, and players with no conscience who don't care who they hurt as long as they get what they want. It will keep you turning pages from the first word to the last. ~ *Regan Murphy, Reviewer*

ROGUE SCION

Shawn Rohrbach

A Black Opal Books Publication

Black Opal Books

BECAUSE SOME STORIES JUST HAVE TO BE TOLD

GENRE: THRILLER/SUSPENSE

ROGUE SCION
Copyright © 2015 by Shawn Rohrbach
Cover Design by Jackson Cover Designs
All cover art copyright © 2015
Author photo by Carlos Mendez
All Rights Reserved
Print ISBN: 978-1-626943-85-8

First Publication: DECEMBER 2015

Published by Black Opal Books **http://www.blackopalbooks.com**

Dedicated to Josh, who never fails to inspire and inform me on the various theories of the New World Order.

CHAPTER 1

The first calls were routine. Three accounts had been drained and the total losses were somewhere in the range of three thousand dollars. This wasn't much to be concerned about, really, for the Sunday morning shift in the call center. The only people really concerned were the yuppies trying to pay for brunch or get some cash out to go mountain biking. The call center was slow otherwise and everyone gathered around the birthday cake.

By noon, there had been fifty more calls, and now the total was near fifteen thousand dollars. Still, no one seemed concerned. People did not talk about it, since each operator had only taken a few of the calls. At break time they started to compare calls and place bets on who would take the call for the greatest amount of lost money.

The manual said to ask the individual if they had given the pin number to someone in the family. That was how it ended normally—a son or cousin admitted to a drug habit, admitted to stealing from the accounts, and the family was in crisis. The best part was the bank didn't have to pay. Once in a while one of those sharp, steely-eyed criminals watched someone key in their pin, knocked them down, and muscled the money out. The cameras on the cash machines caught all that and, if there was a recognizable face, the arrests were fairly routine.

There had been a story in the news about identity theft and how people got pin numbers in various ways. They ended up stealing money from accounts and the bank always blamed it on careless customers. In a few rare cases, the bank paid out money when it was certain it was not the customer's fault. There was never any mention of these. The official line on the website was to teach the customer about identity theft, how to watch for signs of financial abuse in the family, and to keep pin numbers secret.

The cake was gone by noon. Sherry Anne sat back at her station and took the next call. "Northwest Bank and Trust, how can I help you?" she said, wiping chocolate from the corners of her mouth.

"My account. I was trying to withdraw money and it said I had none. That's over twenty thousand dollars."

Sherry Anne smiled and stood up, waving her hands. She flashed all ten fingers twice in the air. Everyone who could see raised their arms in a salute.

"I'm very sorry to hear that, sir. Is there anyone you may know who might have known your personal identification number? Often people will send someone to the store or the bank and give their pin out and then the—"

"My kids don't steal from me, you bitch. I am missing twenty grand. I need that money in my account."

"Sir, I need to take some information down and pass this along to our security department—"

"Just put my money back so I can eat something today."

"Sir, our security department is closed now. When they open, first thing Monday morning, they will have your information and can begin their investigation."

This exchange carried on for twenty minutes and, in spite of the customer's insistence on getting his money immediately, Sherry Anne convinced him the office was closed. He finally cooperated by providing pertinent information. She marked the case "low priority" and noted at the bottom the customer had admitted using the debit card frequently in front of his children. That was for calling her a bitch. She submitted the ticket for Monday review, even though the security office was open and taking cases.

Sherry Anne guessed by the time she arrived at her primary job on Monday morning, the customer would be raving mad and probably very hungry. She scanned the activity of the account. There was a regular automatic deposit of eight thousand three hundred and thirty dollars. Payroll. His take home was three times her gross and he lost twenty grand? She laughed. Then there were the restaurant purchases—one hundred and thirty dollars average. There were liquor store purchases. Lots of gas. She guessed this guy spent more eating out and drinking than she made on both jobs.

She went to get some ice water. The call center was very busy now. Her supervisor stood above her cubicle and yelled for all call center personnel to return to their desks immediately. The calls were put on hold as one customer after another reported five hundred, two thousand, and five thousand dollar thefts from their accounts. The call was made to the Director of Security, Gene Surrey, and he, in turn, called the Bank President, Mary Reichert. They met at the call center and started to print out the intake reports. When it finally slowed at five, more than two thousand customers had called. The total reported loss was over two million dollars. Gene Surrey surmised the thefts were all related. He began retrieving the log of network activity, saying he would begin to piece together a profile and grab pertinent information about the location of the perpetrator. Mary Reichert told him to stop.

"In my office, now." Mary called the shift supervisors into a special meeting. Gene Surrey was asked to leave half an hour into the meeting. Her final words to the supervisors were clear—no one speaks of this to the police or the press until further notice. She called Gene Surrey in and gave explicit instructions for him to speak only to her about any matter in the case. He nodded and left.

The call center had quieted. A few customers who had called earlier tried to gather more information about their lost funds. The operators had nothing to report. It seemed the worst was over. The operators looked sullenly at each other. They were expressly told to say nothing. They were to go home and act as if the event had never happened. They were told there would be more calls, no doubt, because some people who had not tried to access their funds on Sunday would find out on Monday or Tuesday. They were told the nature of the event was so sensitive that speaking about this to anyone might tip off the perpetrator and he would never be caught. They didn't like the instructions but needed the job. The next shift supervisor was advised by Gene Surrey and sent to the floor to manage the swing shift.

Mary Reichert ordered that every customer who had experienced a loss was to receive an immediate cash deposit from the bank of ten percent of the total amount they reported missing. They would be told the investigation was ongoing.

By Monday morning, she had permission from the board of directors to replace all lost funds immediately. She ordered this done and sent a congratulatory email to all staff, commending them on their professionalism and citing this as the main reason the issue was resolved so quickly.

Sam Wilkerson, VP of Operations, abruptly left the call center, dialed a number on his cell phone, and waited. "Grady? I need to talk with you. Fast."

CHAPTER 2

Grady Marcs coiled the rope carefully with long, smooth loops. He liked a rope you could throw over the edge—it would unravel without knots and just hang free and loose. Most climbers didn't pay that much attention to these small details. He did. He learned that a good rope with no tangles or knots was more desirable when under fire. Taking a few extra seconds now could save his life later.

Someone called him anal once. He wasn't anal by the true definition. He was just careful when it came to preserving his life. The laundry could pile up and the coffee cups would sit by the bed for a few days, but when it came to his life, he took precautions. He had seen death and wanted to avoid it.

Grady had insisted on starting at seven, giving them three hours of peace. There were two other climbers, but they were gone in an hour leaving Grady and Sam Wilkerson alone to enjoy the cool, dry morning. It was now ten in the morning and the tourists were beginning to show up. Gary smiled at them as they scrambled over one another to climb the shorter, easier routes in Boulder

City. Most of them were getting ready to climb without helmets. The rest of their gear was over kill for the easy sloping routes they were choosing. By eleven, it was hot and going to get hotter. Grady set the last of the gear in the truck and slammed the door.

There was a lake on the way back that Grady knew of and said it would be a good place to eat some lunch. "Tomorrow, we're going to fish this lake, but today I wanted you to just see it. I've got a fly rod for you to try out."

Sam helped place the two pack sacks into the back of the truck. "I came to work, Grady. I came to get you to work, I mean."

"This is how we work here in Jackson Hole."

The ride to the lake was fairly smooth, until they hit the narrowing access road. Sam knew immediately why no one else did much at the lake. He held tightly to the "oh shit" bar as the truck bounced and slid over boulders the size of pumpkins.

"Not good for the wine, this road." Grady frowned. "I brought something that won't be too damaged. It's not that great, but for a lunch at the lake it'll do fine."

They finally stopped and walked down to the smooth, quiet lake. Across to the East, they could see part of the Grand Tetons, some still capped with snow juxtaposed against the dark blue shy. One small boat sat motionless near the far Southern shore. Other than that, there were no other humans.

"Yeah, this is nice." Sam sat on a large rock. "Grady, I need you to do some work for me."

"God, I hate work. You know that."

"Yeah, you always say that and then you charge me up the ass."

"But I'm good. Very good." Grady opened the wine and let it breathe. "What's up?"

Sam started with the melt down in the call center. He finished with the pay off and then the silence. A crime had been committed and the bank would not admit it. They never called the police. The board of directors, the CEO, and the president just decided to pay everyone back and that was that. All personnel were directed to consider the matter closed and to speak with no one about it.

"You're speaking to me, Sam."

"And I could get fired."

"How much did they take?"

"Two million and change."

"And the potential loss of depositors and commercial customers? Wouldn't that be more like one hundred million?"

Sam wagged his head back and forth. "Maybe. We have insurance for this. We didn't even consider that as an option."

"Come on, Sam. News of a cyber theft of personal accounts at a bank, the bank might as well close its doors."

"But someone got away with two million dollars that does not belong to them."

Grady poured some wine and opened the cheese. "You have a security guy, Gene something."

"Surrey. Gene Surrey."

"What's going on with him? Isn't he investigating this, anyway? He's inside and can keep his lips sealed. What's he found?"

"He's an ass kissing moron. Mary told him to stop investigating it and he did. He ordered everyone in IT and MIS to stay off it, and they do. No one is touching it." Sam tasted the wine and raised an eyebrow. "Nice. This thing just bothers the shit out of me. Someone walks away with two mil and we sit on our thumbs. It could be terrorists, it could finance weapons. Who knows? And we just let two mil walk out the door because we want it hushed up."

Grady ate quietly. "What do you really want me to do here?"

He let Sam organize a response, which he gave to Grady. "The reason I want you to come in is to find them and, yes, it will be very difficult to do this. Gene will want to keep a lid on all of the logs, transfer paths, all of the electronic data for the accounts, everything—you will have to get this information on the QT. Once we have information on what really happened, we need to convince the police a crime and a cover up occurred."

Grady laughed. "You're ready to retire?"

"Yeah, yeah. I thought about that. This is probably suicide, politically. I mean, I should just walk away. I even entertained a new job offer, associate vice president at a competitor's, but I built this fricking bank with my friends, and now this bitch is going to let someone bleed us to death."

Grady ate his lunch in silence and, when he was finished, began to clean up. "I doubt I would be very successful on this one, Sam. I think I need to pass this time."

❦❦❦

"How do I say your name? Is it like Marse? Something like that?"

She meant well and Grady smiled. "It's like the name M-a-r-k-s, just say Marks. That's how you say my name."

"Oh. It looks like Marse."

Now he was irritated. He placed the food in the cooler and checked the fly rods. Everything was ready. He looked at his watch.

It was eight o'clock sharp in the morning and there

was Sam walking out of the hotel dressed in blue jeans, flannel, and a fishing vest.

"Good, you left the tie at home."

"Yeah. Well, my mind won't be much on the fishing. We got hit again last night. Three hundred thousand. She's covering the total amount and mum's the word. Nothing."

"Go to the police."

"With what? My information is coming from a shift supervisor in the call center. She was a teller in the main branch when I was developing the branch managers. I liked her for her honesty and she's always a source of good information. But I can't reveal my source or she's toast, along with me."

"You're concealing a crime."

"I've been ordered to and Mary carries that responsibility."

"You're backing me into this, aren't you?"

"Hey, you keep talking about it, so pretty soon you're an accomplice. You know a crime was committed and you're not doing anything about it, either."

"I'm not an accomplice to anything. I am advising you to go to the police."

"Yeah, with what? Mary doesn't have to show the cops anything. She can say nothing happened. We can hide ten million dollars from the cops and they wouldn't know what they were looking at. What I need is evidence."

Grady started the truck. He drove quietly for a few miles and then looked at Sam. "If I catch my limit today, I'll see what I can do."

Grady had been a member of the army rangers prior to attacks on the World Trade Center. He'd served on a special task force in Northern Afghanistan. His orders were to develop plans and then secretly install telecommunications systems in the country, effectively laying the groundwork for an eventual invasion. After the Russians were run out, the Taliban took over and allowed the country's technical infrastructure to deteriorate to the point that there was no effective telecommunications system in place. Normally, he was sent in to destroy command and control, not to leave a basic infrastructure in place to be used by the conquering army. But military planners decided if there was ever going to be any action against the Taliban and Al-Qaida, they needed a telecommunications system in place. The simple satellite system served the new government well once the Taliban was defeated.

Grady completed his commitment to the rangers in 2005 and resigned his commission. He returned to civilian life to again help run the software company he had founded prior to enlisting. During his absence, it had grown and prospered under the able guidance of his wife, Sandy. They were offered an exclusive buy out, leaving them with enough money to retire to a life of outdoor adventure for him and voluntary public service for her. For pocket money, Grady took on occasional private investigative work. He had no desire to use his killing instincts in this line of work and figured there would be little need for them, but it was nice to know they were there.

He caught his limit. "Damn you, Sam. I'll need some inside information. By the way, did I tell you you're buying dinner?"

CHAPTER 3

Peter never saw himself as a writer. People usually wrote because they needed money, and he didn't. He had access to more money than most people would earn in three life times. He had never worked for a living and never would. He didn't even work to invest the money—his father paid others to do that for him. But he needed to write something now—a warning.

His first attempt was awkward. "This is a message for every freedom loving individual in the world. Read this and be warned. We truly are entering a time of The New World Order. You have heard about it and scoffed at the messengers. They are right and you and your children and the next five generations of your family will soon live in servitude or you will die."

He read it out loud and thought it sounded pompous. Stupid even, like the ranting on the Internet. He deleted the paragraph, closed the laptop, and took a fresh sheet of paper from the drawer. He could write better by hand. He stared for several minutes and set the pen down. He told himself to just tell the story the way it happened. He sipped his drink, picked up the pen, and started writing...

❧❦❧

"The date was October 10, 1992. I was visiting the office of Doctor Joyce Sutton, my psychiatrist at the time. I always just stared silently at Dr. Sutton. My wrists were bound in bandages from my suicide attempt and I tried to scratch under them.

"'Don't scratch those. They will heal faster.' Dr. Sutton leaned back in her large chair and looked me in the eyes. 'I can help you, Peter. You just need to start talking.'

"This was our fourth session and I had every intention of always remaining silent and never talking about why I wanted to commit suicide. My driver always waited patiently for me out in the lobby each time for the hour-long session, wordlessly escorted me to the car, and drove me back home.

"Dr. Sutton was a little anxious that day and told me, 'What happened to you was very traumatic and, for you to get beyond this, we need to talk. I cannot help you until you decide to help yourself.'

"Dr. Sutton specialized in pre-adolescent trauma. I found out later that, after graduating from the California School of Professional Psychology, she decided to treat the children of the wealthy, like me. She had no patience, really, for anyone who could not afford her. I learned also she made a lot of money from the recovered traumatic memory industry. She really liked front-line child trauma of the rich and the money it paid. Rich people did not want their children to grow up weird, and she never promised a cure—just extensive, long-term treatment of the symptoms. This afforded her the co-op overlooking Central Park and a summer place on Fire Island. She seemed surprised one day when I told her how much I knew about her.

"I kept track of our time by the clock. It always chimed on the quarter hour. I recalled looking up at the clock and the swinging pendulum, and Doctor Sutton said something I didn't like.

"I spoke to her for the first time ever right then. 'We have forty-five minutes left. Have you ever seen someone killed?' I gave up trying to pick at the scabs and just flopped my arms on to my lap.

"'Did you?' Dr. Sutton wrote something with her pen. I am sure it was something about did I ever see someone die.

"'I think so.'

"'Do you want to tell me about it?'

"I told her it looked like I had to. I said I knew I was going to keep getting sent over there until she told my father it was okay for me not to come anymore. It seemed like this is what she wanted to hear from me, so I guess I had to talk about it.

"I think coming from a twelve year old boy, this surprised her. 'No one is forcing you to be here,' she said.

"'That's crap.' I laughed and smiled 'So, here we go.'

"I described traveling by plane from New York to San Francisco. Someone met us at the airport like they always did and we drove out of the city and into some woods. I guess it took something over two hours to drive. The car was stopped at a check point, something like I had seen in a movie about the Nazis. Armed guards with guns walked around the car while the driver gave them some papers. The main guard who was giving orders smiled and waved us through. The steel gate lifted and the driver moved slowly along the road through the woods. We came to another guardhouse, but all the men here were dressed in black suits and had sunglasses. This time we all had to get out of the car. The main guy at this checkpoint apologized to my father and told him it was necessary. My father laughed and said it was all okay, no problems. They called my father by his real last name.

"The car was waved through, drove a short distance, and stopped in front of a large cabin. There were several more men in black suits, walking around, making a point to smile at me and my father, nodding at us, but saying nothing. I said I felt scared and sat in my bedroom crying, but I didn't want anyone to know I was crying. My father told me we were going to spend a week at his summer camp and, if I liked it, I could go every year. I didn't want to disappoint my father so I decided to leave my bedroom and ask if there were other boys in the camp I could play with.

"The other summer camp I had been sent to had play areas, organized games, hikes, swimming, and running races and that camp was in Germany. This one was in California

"'Did you like the other camp?' Dr. Sutton seemed bored when she asked and I just smiled at her. She was getting paid to listen and it was obvious she didn't care about my little story. 'We were not allowed to wear clothes at the camp in Germany. They called it a nudist colony.' I smiled again when Dr. Sutton lifted her head back and raised her eyebrows. 'But everyone there was real nice and it was a lot of fun. Not like this place.'

"'I may ask you some questions about that.'

"I had her. She was listening now. 'Like if anyone ever touched me, like, in a bad way? Never happened.'

"We sat staring at each other for a few minutes and I just continued to tell her about being at the new camp.

"My father found a group of boys playing a game of softball and left me there. He spoke to one of the men in suits and that guy nodded at my father. The boys ended the game and we decided to go for a hike up to a swimming hole in the river. I was happy now to be with boys my own age and doing something fun. There were always two or three men either in black suits or in rugged outdoor clothing nearby, talking into radios and staying twenty or thirty feet away from us.

"A few hours later, one of the men shouted at us that it was time to go back to the camp and we all returned as a group, the men in front of and behind us. I told Doctor Sutton I had become accustomed to this. My own father would hire men to watch me, so it didn't seem strange to be watched by so many when there were fifteen or twenty other boys. Some of these men had machine guns strapped over their shoulders and they said nothing to us boys.

"'Did you think these men were going to harm you?'

"I thought that was a stupid question and just shook my head and laughed. 'No, they would have killed anyone who got close to us, we knew that.'

"'Was that what happened, did they have to kill someone who might have looked like he was going to harm you boys?'

"I was getting a little tired of her questions. 'No, my grandfather says that if a bodyguard has to kill someone, he hasn't done his job right and will be immediately fired and probably sent to jail.'

"Dr. Sutton sat back in silence, watching me. The clock chimed on the half hour.

"I smiled and continued. I described an outdoor buffet with every imaginable food and black men in white uniforms serving me on pretty, nice glass plates. Not the nicest. The tables were outside and were all covered with white tablecloths and the silverware was real silver. The glassware was crystal, but not very nice. I ate what I wanted and found my father sitting at a table with some men I saw on television all the time. On television, they were always in suits and, at this camp, they were in shorts and T-shirts and sandals, and I was certain it was the same men. They were all very nice to me.

"My father was drinking a lot of wine and was laughing with the other men. When it got dark, someone came up to our table and said something about relaxing, don't worry, something like that. 'Don't walk fast, but join us.'

"We all walked down a trail toward a lake. At one end of the lake was a large statue. It was really large, like forty feet high. It looked like a bird, maybe an owl, and there were fires burning on the side, not like big fires, but for light. This was when two of the other boys came up to me and asked if I had seen one of the older boys who was like thirteen or something and I told them no. The boys said they were eating together when one of the men in suits came and told the older boy to come with him. He just left his plate and never came back. They asked their dads about the boy and they said they didn't know anything about it. While they were talking about the older boy, a group of people came out from behind the statue dressed in black robes, something like I had seen at a monastery in Germany.

"I stopped here and stared out the window. This is where the story goes ugly.

"Dr. Sutton put her pen down. 'What is it, Peter, What's going on?'

"I was crying now, trying hard to speak between the sobs. 'Well, this boy, this older boy, pushed me when we were at the river and I almost fell in. One of the men grabbed him and took him away from us for a while and then let him return. I think what happened to him was my fault.'

"'How would it be your fault?'

"'My grandfather always tells me we are rich and, if

anyone ever tries to harm us, we will always harm them even worse in return. And this boy pushed me into the river.'

"'So, why do you think something bad happened to him?'

"I gained some control and told Dr. Sutton that some of the men in robes carried a live body wrapped in a white sheet, laying on some kind of bed. The body was the size of the older boy. They started a big fire behind the statue and carried the body back there and, in a few minutes, everyone could hear screaming, real high-pitched screaming, and all the men cheered and cheered.

"I remember I began to hyperventilate and fell on the floor unconscious. I recall waking up and had no idea how long I had been lying on the floor. Dr. Sutton calmly rose from her chair and called the front desk to get medical help right away. She summoned the driver from the waiting room and they both stood over me, watching.

"'He'll be okay, Doctor. This happens. The medics will take him to the hospital and he'll be fine.'

"'Okay.' Dr. Sutton closed her notebook and set it on the desk. 'You'll have him here at ten next Wednesday?'

"'Yes, Doctor. We'll be here at ten.'

"'That's fine. My next client is here and I will be using the other office while you attend to him.'

"The clock chimed on the hour. It is June fifth, two thousand and fifteen, and this is my clearest recollection of when my father brought me to what, I learned later, was called the Bohemian Grove. This was the incident that caused me to want to kill myself at the age of twelve."

Peter set his pen down and sipped his drink.

ఇళ్ళు

It was just a little bomb, but it would shake the sensibilities of the citizens of San Francisco. The target would confuse people and that was fine. Peter would have to help everyone make the connection. It would eventually lead up to the ultimate target and they might see it in the end.

"Oh, yes, that little company making pepper spray was a brick in the foundation of the New World Order."

Bullshit. No one would ever see it, not until he drew a big picture on the wall and told them what they were looking at.

He taped the pipe bomb to the natural gas line and set the timer. He walked away in the dark to the Range Rover. He heard the bomb, but when he watched the news back in his hotel, they barely mentioned it as a natural gas explosion, causing a few thousand dollars in damage. The next morning he drove to Los Angeles.

※※※

The company that made the slippery foam used for crowd control was in a rundown business park in San Bernardino. He taped the bomb to the natural gas line and they also reported it as a natural gas explosion. It was a small company with ten employees. No one was hurt, but Hazmat was called because of the chemicals. No one knew it was a company that made a product used by police to control people, keeping them from exercising their right to gather and speak in public. Again, no one would make the connection until he made it for them.

Hopefully, not before it was too late. He drove to Las Vegas where his forty-five foot motorhome was parked.

※※※

Peter had decided he would miss a few things when

he achieved his goal of stopping the transition from free-dom to mind slave. His brand of single malt scotch, for instance, was expensive and if he was willing to give up the money he had enjoyed so much throughout his life, he would probably not be able to afford it. And there was the skiing—wherever and whenever he wanted anytime of the year. He would surely miss the family compounds on the beach in Tahiti and Sun Valley. He could call one of the family jets any time and, within hours, be on his way anywhere in the world. All of this he would miss, but it would be worth it.

People like his father should be stopped. They did anything they wanted to anyone they chose. It was said they were often so insulated they had no idea what impact their actions had on other people, but that was crap. Sometimes, they picked out the person or persons and gave specific orders. Most often, it was financial or legal problems—send kiddie porn to someone, tell the police, and the man was ruined. Peter had heard his father once talk about faking an identity theft. He stole three million dollars from someone who wouldn't sell him some land and the man never recovered. The family sold him the land after the man committed suicide.

Peter opened the laptop again and logged on to a re-sistance website. He read some of the recent postings. Bull shit. These whiners who bitched about the price of oil were already drones, driving back and forth to work and eating crappy food year after year until they retired. Then they could barely afford to travel and, after a few years, they would be dead because of shitty medical care. He laughed again. The last posting he read caught his at-tention.

...cut their balls off, steal their money, and they will lose the one tool they have to control us.

He sipped from the scotch and replied, *You seem like*

a sincere person, but you have no clue what it would take to steal enough money to make a difference in their lives. I can barely believe you would write something as spurious as this. This is like trying to take out Goliath with a spit wad. He added his email address to the posting.

He flipped over to an inventory of explosives to account for the product he had just used. There was enough left stashed in the motorhome to make an impact somewhere. Add fifty-one gallon jugs of gas and Oklahoma would look like a fire cracker. A mechanized voice told him he had an email from PowderGirl. It opened automatically.

Douche, who the fuck are you to lecture me? Screw off.

Peter replied, *When you make statements that truly indicate you know nothing of the monetary structure that protects the elite, you lose all credibility. You would never even find their money, let alone the people who control it. Good luck, PowderGirl.* After sending it, he went to pee.

As he refreshed his ice and scotch, there was a loud screech coming from the speakers on his computer and then a woman's voice yelled, "I can find anyone I want. Fuck you."

The computer shut off and Peter was not able to reboot.

CHAPTER 4

Melissa Eggers was late. This was rare, but she had her neighbor, Mike Spangler, to thank. He was face down on the ground as the San Diego County Sheriff SWAT team yelled at him to place his hands behind his back. Mike's house was the smallest on the block and it never surprised Melissa when there was trouble. Small house, small bank account, trouble. Simple as that. They quickly shoved him into the back of a cruiser and the police began to hang yellow crime scene tape around his house. Melissa pointed at the cruisers in her driveway. They were moved slowly as the police chose to carry on with their arrest rather than let her get her car out.

She arrived at the base and presented her badge and identification at the gate. The young marine saluted stiffly and waved her through. She parked in front of the base commander's office.

She was dressed in a conservative black two-piece suit with a white blouse, her long black hair flowing as she walked lively up the stairs. Heads turned. She was a striking figure, compared with the mostly male population dressed in drab military green and tan uniforms.

Colonel Jerry Bartle was sitting behind his desk, holding a cup of steaming coffee in his favorite titanium mug. Melissa waved at his secretary and entered the room. She shut the office door and pulled a red folder from her briefcase. "Sorry I'm late, Colonel. My neighbor invited the San Diego County SWAT team to his house this morning." Bartle didn't smile. "You have someone on base using your computer system to send base secrets to a little known terrorist cell in Spain. They are not Spanish, but the language of choice is Spanish and they seem to operate from there. I have isolated the computers that have been used. They are the public access computers in the PX and the mess. Since there is no log in required, there is very little I can do to pin point who it is right now. Do you have security cameras in these areas?"

Colonel Bartle sipped the coffee slowly, looking directly at her. "Yes, but I doubt they will show who has been using those computers. You know, I requisitioned fifty more security cameras and I got nothing. So much for Homeland Security." He paused. "I thought I ordered to have those computers locked down tighter than a nun's you know what. No one is supposed to be able to upload anything. They are Internet access only, read only. Nothing more. No email, nothing."

"In theory, sir, you are right. It can appear that these are locked down just as you say, but anyone with half an education in computer science can easily find a way—"

"Yeah, yeah. Explain this to me in layman's terms."

"Well, sir, you see that flash drive you have plugged into your computer? A smart guy could put an operating system on it, say like Linux, it's kind of like Unix. If I have the ability to change the boot order of the computer, or if I'm lucky and the operating system on the computer just let me do it, I can run the operating system on the flash drive and take control of the computer and basically do anything I want. Now, there are some things the guy would have to do, but that's one easy way in a nutshell."

He set the coffee down and picked up his phone. "Would you ask Major Screwup, I mean Major Markum to find it in his heart to get his sorry ass into my office right now? Thank you." He slammed the phone down. "Advise me."

"I would recommend very discreet surveillance. The transmissions have become a little more frequent and, based on the pattern I saw, I can easily predict that within the next two days or so this person or these people will attempt it again. I can actively monitor traffic. We can associate activity with an individual and we will have a date and time stamp—"

"Make it so." He waved Major Markum into his office. "Major, you know Ms. Eggers."

"Yes, sir." The major held out a large, manicured hand.

"Well, you know those computers I told you to lock down. Guess what. They're being used to transfer base secrets to terrorists."

"That's not possible, sir."

"Really." Colonel Bartle sat back behind his desk. "Ms. Eggers, unless you want to hear me use extremely profane language, I advise you to leave and make necessary arrangements to find this scum bag. I need to have a private word with my major." He smiled and waved at Melissa. "My security officer will be expecting you."

CSCS

The military consulting contract was lucrative. The nasty business at MIT never came up in the background check. She always wondered why, but figured someday someone would show up on the Internet, looking for money and try to extort her. Good luck. Besides, she figured by then she would have succeeded in squirreling away enough money, the event would be nothing more than an embarrassment to MIT and never affect her at all.

She pulled the Lexus into the parking lot of the small city library and waited in a line for several minutes until a computer was available. She booted around the library log in screen and set up a ping of a public IP address. She liked to think of the Northwest Bank and Trust as the Better Bank for Melissa. The port she wanted was open. She wondered how morons got information security jobs and did exactly the opposite of what they should have been taught to secure a network. From memory, she typed in user names and passwords of six accounts and transferred money to four accounts with dynamic account numbers. It was a small take, just under ten thousand dollars.

She ended the session and rebooted the computer, smiling at the two patrons waiting in line. "Happy computing."

CHAPTER 5

Gene Surrey did everything you would expect from a short, ambitious man. He talked loud, walked hard, and demanded perfection from everyone else, in an attempt to hide his own glaring faults. He looked down at the spots on his tie as he walked. He sat at the conference room table, looking out the window, ignoring Grady and Sam. The view was of Lake Union with all of the house boats lined up along the shore.

Grady had known Gene from his ranger years when Gene was a civilian contractor. Gene helped write some of the initial firmware for the Trojan Spirit I and then the Trojan Spirit II telecommunications systems used as a vehicle-mounted forward-deployed all-in-one telecommunications system, allowing commanders of various branches a secure and easily deployed system. He had been assigned to write the same code for the Trojan Spirit Lite, the smaller version modified to be transported on a truck or via helicopter to very forward positions. Grady was instrumental in designing the operating system and needed Gene's work to interface with the hardware. Gene was axed from the team and replaced immediately when he was caught chatting in a bar about the code he was writing. An investigation determined he had violated a few laws, but the recipient of the information was cleared for secret, not for top secret. Both were reprimanded and Gene was never allowed to work on government projects again.

He liked to lie about this. He would claim he belonged to a special projects unit developing spyware that was going to take out the Iranian nuclear program. When confronted with the reality that the Israelis and some programmers located in the United States had already done this, he would laugh it off and say that was a ruse to keep the Iranians away from the truth. Another version of the lie was a story about a system that collected information on every citizen of the United States and used a predictive model to determine who would commit a crime and stop them before it ever happened. He would deny there was a popular television program with exactly that plot. To get his job at the bank, he'd turned to his first cousin, Mary Reichert, who decided having family around in this capacity would help her control things better.

In front of Gene was a four-inch binder filled to capacity. Mary Reichert entered the room ahead of her executive assistant, who persisted in talking even after Mary sat down. Mary smiled and waved her away. She read a log report in silence, looking up occasionally to smile thinly and then go back to her reading. "Sam tells me you might be able to help us."

Grady breathed deeply, waiting for Gene to face them at the table. Gene kept looking out the window at the bright summer sky. "Perhaps. I only have bits and pieces of what is going on. If you could fill me in a little better, then maybe I can offer my services or just decide we are wasting each other's time."

"Gene, can you give Mr. Marcs some details."

Gene continued to stare out the window and sighed. He opened the binder and began to read log entries out loud. He was giving date and time stamps of intrusion attempts at the perimeter firewall and then, several minutes later, read from a list the account numbers, the names of the account owners, and the dollar amounts that had been taken. After twenty minutes, he stopped and looked at Mary. "Is that helpful?"

Grady stared across the table. "Not really."

Gene flashed a scowling glance at him.

"I'm sorry, but Gene, you told me this morning this was the information Mr. Marcs would need, Mary said. "Mr. Marcs, what else might be helpful?"

"I would like to see a couple of things. First, I would like to see a logical diagram of your system architecture with emphasis on your firewall. I would also like to see configuration documentation of the firewall and all security appliances from that point inward. Finally, I would like to see your perimeter security policy."

"Absolutely not." Now Gene glared directly at Grady. "Who do you think I am?"

"I would also like to see a chart of the incidents and I want to use that to look for patterns."

"This is insane. We can handle this internally. We are close to finding this person ourselves. We don't need some hot-shot gun for hire to come in here and stick his big nose in our security. That's probably how this whole thing happened—someone on the inside being given access to this information. There is no way you are getting any of this from me." Gene slammed the note book closed. "If you interfere in my internal security, I have high-level connections in Homeland Security and you will be answering to them, hopefully from Guantanamo." He stomped hard out of the conference room.

Mary Reichert was not smiling, but she wasn't angry

either. "Well, I need to give my chief security officer some latitude in preserving the security of the bank."

Sam sat with his hands folded on the table. There was a long silence and then he breathed in to speak. "I spoke with Charles this morning." He looked at Grady. "Charles Greely is the Chairman of the Board for the bank. He founded the bank with me and the others who were originally here." He looked back at Mary. "Charles feels that we need to go forward with an internal investigation with someone who is truly capable of discovering who is doing this—a third party with no personal ties to the security team. He agrees that it should be an internal matter, but is open to bringing in the police at a later point. This was a stipulation Grady made when I first approached him—"

He stopped speaking as a tall, elderly man entered the conference room.

"Mary."

"Charles, how nice." Her tone was flat.

Charles reached across the table, offering his hand to Grady. "Mr. Marcs, I am Charles Greely." He sat down. "Sam told me some things about you and I checked them out. It seems you have a pretty good reputation with the FBI. They are impressed with the work you have done for them in the past, as well as Army Intelligence."

"I get work where I can."

"Indeed. I was listening in as you detailed what you might need before you continue. Mr. Surrey has served us well in certain matters, but I think he is over his head on this one. Mary, please see to it Mr. Marcs receives the information he needs to make a decision, will you?"

Now she was unhappy.

"Mr. Marcs, please contact me directly any time you like." Charles stood, gently pushed a business card across the table, then quietly left the room.

c/ɔc/ɔ

The diagrams were not up to date. Some of the equipment noted on them had been removed and there were now five more servers not noted in any detail. The firewall configuration documentation did not exist. The network administrator was brought in and he recalled from memory the original configuration.

He had to trace back on four occasions and recall how they had changed that over the four years since it had been installed.

The security policy was a one-page document signed by new employees, promising not to use the Internet to search for pornography or gambling sites.

Grady leaned back in his chair. "Do you allow employees to use Instant Messaging?"

"Sure." The network administrator appeared to be in his early twenties. He was over six feet tall, had long shaggy hair, and wore blue jeans that had not been washed in a while. "By the way, I'm Jeffrey."

"Is it encrypted?"

"No." Jeffery laughed quietly. "People here would not know what to do if we encrypted things. They would have to decrypt everything and they would bitch like hell."

"What kind of information do you allow to pass through the messaging?"

"Anything, I guess. The loan officers use it a lot to get information from customers."

Grady said nothing. He rocked in the chair for a while. "You seem like a smart guy, Jeffrey. Are you aware of how terribly insecure this system is?"

"Have you met my boss? I am not going to say anything. I do as I am told and keep looking for a new job."

"That's fair. If I take this on, I am going to need

someone with access afterhours. Could you be of assistance, and yes, I have met your boss. My first recommendation to Charles Greely will be to fire him."

"Dude, I'll help you any way I can. I don't want to see Gene fired, but if that's what the big guy wants..." Jeffrey shrugged and stood up. "Use this email. It's my private one"

Jeffery left to work in the server room and Grady stayed in the conference room reading.

Sam slipped in and nodded quietly. "You found anything?"

"No. There's no way Gene could ever find anyone who gained access to your system. It's so bad, the network administrators can see all of the passwords set by employees or even set by customers in plain text. Anyone who gained access to this network, legitimately or otherwise, had that access. This is the first thing we need to change but, in order to catch this person, we need to let him think we haven't changed a thing. This needs to be done immediately."

Sam used the phone in the conference room to call Charles, spoke a few lines, listened, and then hung up. "Charles says to do whatever you need and just keep him informed."

෴

"It's called a honey pot. Use the same IP address as you had on that server and set it up with a lot of dummy data and fictitious customer accounts. Use the same employee names, but don't put any real data in their accounts." Grady stepped over several boxes and slipped on a pile of fast food bags. He righted himself and stood in front of the server. "Then use this configuration for your real servers, and you see where the passwords are visible in plain text? Just hit that button right there and you have hidden passwords."

Jeffery nodded. "Sorry about the mess, man. I clean up and Gene trashes the place in a few days. I hope you don't think I didn't know how to configure our system to hide passwords. I know it's that easy. I have been looking for a new job because I know how bad this is."

"You said that already. I know what you can do. I know what Gene is capable of as well. Let's not worry about him right now. Let's get this screwed down tight and then try to catch whoever did this."

CHAPTER 6

The new laptop cost three thousand dollars. The cost of repairing the old one would have been minimal, but the memory of the event so haunted Peter, he no longer wanted it. He gave it to the owner of the small computer shop and ordered the new one to be built up. He used the public library to read his email and to search for information on his favorite subject—the impending doom that would destroy us all, known as The New World Order. He didn't like the library. People were always looking over his shoulder to see what he was reading, like they were trying to see if he was some kind of porn freak and exposing kids in the library to it. He could also smell them.

It would have been so easy to leverage his last name into some really nice hotel and borrow one of their computers in his room but the word would get out and he would be mobbed with people trying to get his father's attention. It would just take a phone call to be back in the fold. The lawyers had always told him to use the credit cards, driver's licenses, and other identification they had prepared for him using a different last name, but he re-

fused. Most commoners knew his family name and knew
they had money, but they had absolutely no idea really
how much they had. He was always amused when people
asked if there could be anybody wealthier than Bill Gates.

Peter didn't comprehend the significance of wealth
until he was fifteen. He had always taken for granted that
his grandfather and then his father took calls day or night
from the most powerful people in the world. As a young
boy, when he played with the grandsons of the Queen of
England, he had no clue who they were or what family
they were really from. All he could recall was fighting for
some toys. When he later understood who they were, he
began to realize who he was.

He watched curiously as the boys and their father
now fought with the press, their every motion photo-
graphed, and the entire world wanting to know every
juicy detail of their personal lives. He was horrified by it
and was thankful he could live anonymously, simply by
not giving out his last name. He felt sorry their lives were
devoted to the service of their country, while he would
inherit far more money than they would and he could live
behind the veil.

He hated publicity, a trait he admired so much in his
grandfather. His father, however, loved public admira-
tion, only to see the family name soiled with lies and ex-
tortion attempts when he lived too much in the public
eye.

People did not understand this kind of life. They
didn't comprehend how easy it would be for him to access four or five billion dollars to buy a business or found
a charitable organization. In fact, the lawyers and his father would like him to do just that. Do something. Anything.

And he would. It was just that they were not going to
like it.

ⲥⲟⲥⲟ

"The wireless works fine. I transferred all of your files over from the old hard drive." The technician handed him he receipt and some documentation. "You say it was a gal who sent this thing to you?"

Peter nodded. "She was making these really stupid comments on a forum I participate in and I flamed her so she sent that thing to me."

"Well, she left a trail. Here's a print out of the code for that virus. She's pretty smart, but she wanted to leave a calling card."

"Down in San Diego. I was just there. I might drive down and look her up. So the other computer works?"

"Yeah. I feel bad not giving you some money for it. It's a slick machine."

"Don't worry, one of my father's corporations owns the company. I got it for free."

"I transferred your bookmarks over as well so you won't have to look up your websites again." The technician paused, maybe waiting for some kind of reaction. "I was wondering about that one site, the thing about the one world government and the reptilians. That's some pretty bizarre shit. I read a lot of the book that guy has online. I don't know what I think, but a lot of what he says seems to be true. But super-rich people who can shape shift into reptiles? I don't know, that seems a little whacked to me."

"I find it entertaining." Peter picked up the computer, slid it into the carrying bag, and waved goodbye.

ⲥⲟⲥⲟ

He rolled the Range Rover on to the trailer behind the motorhome. He ate a small dinner and started driving

after ten. He was idling at a stop light just off Interstate
15 by three-thirty in the morning. The drive to Carlsbad
went smoothly with no traffic. He was followed twice by
police, but they pulled away.

By four, he was parked a block away from 6728
Manchester Boulevard. He looked like every other motorhome tourist parked near the beaches. He slept for several hours, waking to the sound of several large motorcy-
cles roaring by on the street.

He made coffee and sat in the passenger seat watching the house. A black Lexus pulled slowly into the
driveway and a tall, black-haired woman got out and entered through the front door. He drank the coffee slowly
and, after half an hour, picked up the printout of the virus
code and stepped out of the motorhome. He walked slowly to the front door of the woman's house and knocked.
He waited for almost a minute before the dead bolt was
unlocked and the door opened.

"Yes, can I help you?"

"You left this on my computer. That was really
messed up, lady." He handed her the print out and walked
away. The look in her eyes was worth the drive.

"Excuse me? What are you talking about?"

He stopped at the edge of the yard. "You are Melissa
Eggers, aka Powder Girl. You sent me a virus when I told
you how stupid you were for your posting on bringing
down the banks. I should call the police, but now I know
where you live."

She stared at him, silent. "Well, as you discovered it
was a temporary thing. Obviously you got the computer
to work. I never intended to do any permanent damage,
and I did want you to find me." She stepped out on to the
front porch. "And was it you who found this?"

"Nope, a tech up in Las Vegas found it. I bought a
new computer from him and gave him that one. "

She walked over to stand in front of him. "You were pretty rude."

"You were being ignorant."

"I've been reading your postings and you seem to know quite a bit about the people who own these conglomerates. We should talk. Where are you staying?"

Peter pointed to the motorhome.

ფ৩ფ৩

She let him park the motorhome on the street in front of the house. They talked for two hours, mostly about each other and how they came to realize it was time take back control of their own destinies and not be controlled by corporate conglomerates. They both lied—she about being expelled from MIT and him about his medications. He also lied about who he really was. He decided he might tell her later about the family, but never about the meds. Whenever he mentioned the meds, they always went away.

She believed that he had a degree in Economics. He had a strong command of the monetary system, much of which she was aware of, but a lot she had never heard. He was careful to distance himself from any personal relationship with the people he referred to as the super wealthy. He had fabricated an intricate story that explained his ability to be just about anywhere he wanted. It had something to do with a short and difficult, but extremely lucrative career at Microsoft. When she said he didn't look older than twenty eight, which was his exact age, he lied and said he was about to turn thirty five.

They soon realized, and admitted, that their respective strategies were not going to make much of an impact. His bombs would make the news and little more. He might be caught, but secretly he knew with his family's lawyers and his medical condition, nothing would happen to him. She could go on stealing from consumer accounts, which were covered by insurance, and never make any significant impact on the march toward total domination. She would be a cyber thief, maybe get some time in prison, and the system would continue to churn on toward total domination of the world. But they both agreed they had to try.

"I just want to hurt at least one of the thirteen blood lines." Melissa looked at him, smiling. "You know what I am talking about, right?"

"Most people really don't know a thing about what they loosely call the Illuminati. There are really about five hundred families, maybe a thousand by now, a few I know you have never heard of, who have an interest in controlling the economies of the world. And they have the money. I am so amused when I read these books and websites, trying to describe my life. The only part they get right is that we have money and we want to control things. After that, it's all just bad guessing. They have no clue and my family will never show them."

"But what about the mind-control slaves?"

He thought it sounded like she was having fun with him. "Never seen one, have you?" He laughed. "Now I take that back. I see millions of them, but they are slaves to their own self-made dreary lives. They get themselves into so much debt, they will never know financial security. And the ones who are running around flaunting twenty or thirty million dollars, they're even more enslaved. They are constantly in fear of losing it. Thirty million dollars is not enough money to control much of anything. They can control family and a few friends and occasionally a crooked politician, but their sphere of influence is really insignificant. And the problem is it's not this highly organized plan to turn everyone into mindless slave drones. We hardly have a common name for it. It's an idea we all share. We will control the money, and that will control world events. We control macro and micro economies as we see fit. We would like to see the same economy from Northern Canada to Argentina, and we are well on our way to achieving that. We see making more money with one static working class economy, first in the Western Hemisphere, and then worldwide. Economy of scale. Wal-Marts everywhere selling millions and millions of things, and factories the world over paying exactly the same minimum wage. We love it when we hear those bigots on television talk about the Mexicans illegally working in the United States taking jobs away. My father is convinced that, in his lifetime, they will be cleaning the pools alongside the Mexicans and a few corporations will own all the homes in America."

"Your family actually talks like this?"

"Yes."

"So, the Illuminati is not a well-organized group of men sitting at the Bilderberg Group, or the Trilateral Commission plotting for a one world government?"

"My grandfather was invited to that meeting once and he just shrugged it off. He said it was mostly a lot of old gas bags who thought they had some influence. You know who is pushing that conspiracy? It's the Christians. I read these websites and they all have a different approach. It's either the New Age religions and the banks, or it's the gays and the banks, or it's the thirteen families using the gays and the New Age religions. And I haven't even started on the Jewish conspiracy theories. These people have too much time on their hands and too little money. I can tell you my family is very amused by it all. We just want economic control in our favor and we have the billions required to achieve just that."

Peter spoke about the summers he spent with Diana's

boys, not knowing who they were then, but later skiing with them in Switzerland when the two families met up. Melissa didn't believe this. Peter offered to show her some photographs. She recognized a few people. The fact that he was in most of the pictures, especially a few of the more recent ski vacations, began to convince her he was at least somewhat truthful.

"What's your last name?"

Peter laughed. "No. It's better you don't know that for now."

"So why are you stabbing the family in the back?"

"Yeah, it usually gets around to that. When I was a kid, I had a sister. We did everything together. Hikes, bike riding, skiing, swimming—everything. We had a great life. She disappeared one day, never saw her again, and my family never spoke a word about her. She was thirteen and I was eleven. When I was eighteen and was being told about the money, the family business interests, and my trust, my mother came down with cancer. When no one else was around, she confided in me that they had my sister put away and, eventually, she died. She was mildly retarded. I think there's a better way of saying that, but it's the term my family uses. They just got rid of her and there was no explanation or investigation of her death.

"I was quiet about this for several years after my mother died. I tried to finish getting a college degree, but I was just so caught up in hatred of my family, I dropped out. I convinced my father I needed to travel so he bought me that motorhome, which I think cost like four million dollars. He told me the jets were available anytime I needed to fly anywhere. He said I would get over it and, when I was ready to continue the family business, I was welcome back any time." Peter collected the photographs and placed them back in the black portfolio. "I have never gotten over it and I never will."

CHAPTER 7

From the bell tower you could see the Mulege River. The small white church was in decent repair, cared for by both the locals and Americans who wintered there. The walls were bright, clean, and adorned with modern Catholic symbols. Even the floor was covered with new gray stone, the grout freshly clean and white. A large, bearded priest entered the church and quietly greeted the older ladies, clutching rosaries, in the first five rows. The candles were lit. Smoke swirled pleasantly up and then disappeared, the smell of the beeswax familiar and certain. There was going to be a Mass, even if it was attended only by old ladies and the priest.

Dressed in a white cassock and a decorated red stole, the priest, his hands held piously together in front of his chest, approached the small stone alter, kissed it, and turned to smile at the ladies. He recited the formal prayers of greeting, of contrition, and of belief in the Word of the Lord, the ladies responding on cue with the scripted prayers in their books. No one was there to assist, so the priest was alone in reading the scriptural passages. The ladies stood for the Gospel and the priest read in his booming, theatrical voice about the parable of the prodigal son. He finished the passage and the ladies sat. This priest, unlike all of the others these ladies had ever known, was always good for a rousing sermon, even on weekday mornings. He paused, wiping his massive hand down his beard, and then hid his hands inside the cassock.

In effortless, if slightly accented Spanish he began, "I never understood this parable. The older son stays home, works his tail off, gets nothing. The younger one, takes part of the inheritance, parties till the wee hours, goes broke, runs back to Daddy, and Daddy throws him a party. The older, hard-working son refuses to go to this party and the father reprimands him. We are told this is supposed to be a story of redemption. I wonder if the barkeepers association didn't write the interpretation of this parable."

The ladies laughed and looked at each other, not at all disappointed by the sermon.

"Here, give your irresponsible son all of your money up front, no contingencies, and we know what he's going to do. We have special liquors and women for just such an occasion. These young fools and their money are soon parted and we put it in our banks."

The ladies laughed again and the priest paused, smiling.

"Of course I am joking. This is one of the more difficult parables because it is about an irresponsible son who wastes his inheritance and comes back to beg forgiveness. The father forgives. And Jesus forgives. Our Heavenly Father forgives. Not very many of you fine ladies would turn away your son who found himself in a similar situation, no? This whole notion of forgiving the prodigal son is at the very core of what it is to be Christian. If we are nothing but industrious, callous, hardwork-

ing, and careful with our money, we do not have the heart
of Jesus in us, we do not have His love. I like the example of the father who was able to acquire some level of
comfort and wealth and not only gave freely to the son
who wasted the money, but accepted him back when he
was lost and suffering. Wealth is not the problem here.
What is the real problem is the judgment heaped on the
younger son by the elder. He sees his sibling as the rogue
scion, the runaway who brings shame and poverty to this
great family. He is nothing but human and the father is
going to love him no matter what he has done with the
money. The bitterness and avarice in the elder son's
stone-cold heart is the problem here."

The church went silent before the priest turned back
to his chair to sit. After a few minutes of reflection, the
Mass continued in Latin. The ladies lined up in single file
to receive their communion wafers, each one sticking out
their tongues instead of taking it in their hands like modern Catholics. The priest obliged. He blessed them and
they began to leave, passing by the small tattered basket
with several pesos in it already to remind the ladies this
was how the priest lived. He hears a few clinks of coins
and nods approvingly. It wouldn't be much, but a fun
well-spoken sermon always got something.

He doused the candles, cleaned the chalice, and
locked the sacramental wine in the small safe in the ves-
tibule. Through the open window he smelled the morning
heat. It was only eight -thirty and already hot. His stomach rumbled for breakfast and he decided that, since his
wife was away, he would just stop and eat somewhere on
his way back to the house.

The locals talked about the priest who had a wife, not
bothered really, but just talked like they talked about the
weather. He sat and nodded at Rosarita. She knew what
to bring him. First the coffee and then the juevos with

extra chilies. He ate slowly, drinking two cups of coffee. A copy of the *New York Times* sat on the shelf. The priest picked it up and read as he ate the scramble eggs. He motioned for another cup of coffee and continued to read. He gestured that he wanted the paper and Rosarita waved him away. He thanked her and then paid.

The walk up the slight hill to the house was now hot and he sweated under the black shirt and slacks. From the outside, the house was unassuming, hidden behind walls, courtyards, and numerous trees. It appeared humble, the house of the priest—as it should be—but, in the garage, the Mercedes suggested a less-humble life. The shade around the pool was a welcome relief. He removed the shirt and sat in a T-shirt to cool down. Martin brought him iced tea and he sipped for a few minutes then unlocked the large steel door along the side of the house. Today, like every Tuesday, his chore was to clean his weapons.

CHAPTER 8

Grady liked early Sunday mornings. No one ever called and he could work as much as he liked. In the early days, when he was coding their first product, he would drive down to Mass at around six. After watching the last of the Saturday night revelers stagger home, he would go to the office, code until four or five in the afternoon, and meet Sandy at her mother's for dinner.

He enjoyed her mother, Glenda, and her strong political views. Sandy would roll her eyes and clear the table, but Grady would stay on, listening to the wisdom and insight of this frail old woman. He was most interested in how the family had built up and maintained one of the last independent lumber yards in Seattle. They sold the yard, only to watch it dissolve under the competition of the big-box home repair places. She bought the company back and maintained control, until she could no longer walk, then turned it over to her son. It was thriving now as a premier source of building materials to the same construction companies that had sustained them for years. He knew where Sandy got her drive and acumen for running their business while he was away serving in the rangers.

But Sunday morning brought him back to the days when he had to struggle. No one else worked on Sundays. They were all out, eating bad over-priced brunches. He had known the day would come when he would not need to work, and this was now a reality. He could pay cash for everything, including the two houses they now owned.

After the six o'clock Mass, he drove to the bank. This time of year it was light for the early Mass, still wet and misty, but at least light. He stopped for coffee.

When he got to the bank, Jeffrey was waiting for him, offering more coffee. "No thanks. Stopped after Mass."

"Mass, huh? I was raised an Episcopalian. Gave it up in high school. Organized religion doesn't do much for me."

"My wife was an Episcopalian until, like she says, she became a Christian. We met after that. Eighteen years of marriage, and we're still together."

"Any kids?"

"One. He's fifteen. And that's the end of the personal questions." Grady squinted kindly at Jeffrey.

"Dude, didn't mean to pry or anything."

The router Grady had asked for was still in the box. He drew a diagram of where he wanted the router placed in the system. He wrote out a lengthy access control list and placed Gene's name in the 'denied access' category. "We're going to monitor all abnormal traffic. Since you really have no traffic that is coming in, any inbound traffic will be considered abnormal."

Jeffrey scratched his head. "Well, that's not quite true. See, Gene snoops on people a lot. I am telling you this now because it won't take you long to discover it. He doesn't know I know because he thinks I am an idiot. But he monitors email, personal documents, web surfing, that sort of thing. Not for everyone, but just the president, the chairman, the board of directors. I'm sure he thinks it will guarantee him a job if they ever decide to cut back."

Grady laughed. "So someone is ripping you off blind and he can't find that person, but he can sniff out the good stuff on his bosses."

"That pretty much sums it up."

As Jeffrey placed and configured the router, Grady called Charles Greely. He explained what Gene was doing. He further explained how he could monitor Gene and save the data into a log. Charles asked him to do it and tell no one else.

Grady observed the network traffic, watching Gene accessing email accounts. He began to wonder if Gene was not perhaps involved with the thefts. Usually, a man who insisted that he was the only really trustworthy and secure person in the company turned out to be the most deceptive cracker in the system. It often went like that. The morning passed and the only intrusion activity was Gene's. Grady logged the data and configured an auto sensor that would send an alert to him and Jeffrey on their cell phones if there was any different kind of intrusion.

He gave Jeffrey remote access to the router and, when he was comfortable with Jeffrey's ability to log any activity remotely, Grady was ready to leave.

"If anything jumps out at us, monitor the activity until it ends. If they are in the system for more than thirty seconds, my trace route app will know exactly which computer they used. Since this is not being reported as a crime, all we can do is log the data and show it to Charles."

උත්තර

Grady arrived at Glenda's in time to sit down to pot roast and apple pie. Sandy chided him for being late. He set his laptop on the coffee table in the living room. He knew the neighbors to either side of the house had installed unsecured wireless for their homes. If a call came, he would be able to monitor it from there. There was no call. Instead, he was able to relax. Grady and Grady Junior cleared the table and washed the dishes. All cleaned up, they sat at the table with Glenda to play canasta until Sandy decided it was time to leave. Grady pulled a crisp twenty from his wallet. He actually owed Glenda twenty two dollars and said he would have to pay her next week. She shook her head and snatched the twenty from his hand. "I told you not to marry this skin flint. Can't even pay his gambling debts."

"I wouldn't owe you anything if you didn't cheat all the time."

☙☙☙

The call came at midnight. Grady was already at his desk and quickly logged into the bank information system. Jeffrey was in before he was. They watched the perpetrator access five accounts, taking a little more than three thousand dollars. This didn't take any more than sixty-five seconds. Whoever was doing this was good, Grady thought, but not good enough to avoid leaving behind footprints.

He had the MAC and IP address, the Internet service provider, the account number of the recipient, and the fact it was a mobile broadband service. The perpetrator was currently sitting near the beach in Carlsbad, California. Jeffrey called when he saw this same data. "I want a copy of that program, dude."

"Yeah. We'll see. Can you be at the bank by six-thirty or so? I know it's after midnight, but I want to have you there when Mary and Gene show up."

"Yeah, sure, as long as you tell the old man how great I'm doing and I get some comp time down the road."

"We'll see how great you're doing."

ぐぐぐ

Mary and Gene were told they would be reviewing log files of the theft activity but, in reality, they were looking at the log files of Gene's snooping that Grady had compiled. Charles Greely sat calmly at the middle of the table. The only sound came from the paper as they turned the pages.

Mary closed the log file and pushed it away. "I'm not sure what the significance of this is, Charles."

"Mary, how long have I known you? Five years? I personally recruited you. I saw huge potential in you. I was right. You have written more commercial paper for us than your predecessor could have imagined. It was the right choice bringing you on, until lately." Charles drummed the table with his long fingers. "It's bad enough that Gene here has been viewing your classified emails to me and the members of the board, but now that I can read them and also the emails you have been sending to BOA with sensitive data, I am beginning to see that you would rather be there than here. I am offering you the opportunity to do just that. As for you Gene, you are fired as of this moment. Security is waiting outside the door to escort you to your desk and then out. Mary you have until the end of the day." Charles stood and walked out of the room.

CHAPTER 9

Melissa sat staring at the computer. She knew someone had detected her, but they did nothing to stop the transfers. She knew she had left a footprint, but this was not the kind of detection system she normally saw when the police set up their own monitoring. They had to play by the rules or the evidence was useless, but this one was definitely thinking outside the box. She had seen something like this only during her MIT days and a classmate had written a tracer. She had used Peter's laptop to show him how easy it was to get the money and so they could never trace it to her unless of course they arrested Peter and he started crying. Even then, they wouldn't have evidence. Regardless, she would never transfer money out of Northwest again.

She knew what to do, even at MIT—she always used a public-access computer and someone else's account, whenever possible, without them knowing it. In a pinch, she got a fenced laptop, found public wireless access, took the money, and disposed of the computer—usually in a dumpster. She knew how not to leave an electronic footprint.

They never filed charges because they had no solid evidence, but she had been expelled.

To fight the expulsion, she might have given up evidence, so she walked away. It only returned to haunt her once when one employer actually called the registrar's office and asked. All MIT could say was she had been expelled. It could have been for any violation of the rules of conduct, something minor. She didn't get that job and it didn't matter. That was the other lesson she learned— be able to just walk away. Besides, there were more banks just as inept at security as Northwest.

Peter's reaction to the transfers was one of amused disdain. "I can spend more than that when I buy clothes. These transfers, as you call them, will do nothing. It might give you a few nice meals, but my father, alone, has more assets than that bank and five other regional chains of banks combined. And what my grandfather still controls is substantially more than that, and we are just one family. Are you beginning to understand?" Peter poured some more wine. "Tomorrow morning, I can call my family's attorneys and tell them I need ten million dollars for some real estate investing I want to undertake. It is such an insignificant amount of money they will not ask any questions. They will simply ask which one of my accounts I want the money in. Now, that might seem to you a fairly serious transaction, but actually my father would be pleased if I asked for the money for any business venture. I will never be held accountable for it, and they will never ask what I did with it. That's money."

Melissa hated the wealthy, even this arrogant, handsome bastard sitting across the table from her. "So to really get them, instead of transferring money, why not simply cut off access."

"How do you mean?"

"It's the same principle as your little bombs. You

deny people access to businesses that contribute to the takeover by corporate conglomerates. But instead of blowing up a building that will be replaced next week, why not destroy the money instead of taking it."

"You mean blow up a bank?"

"No. Money is mostly electronic. It is a binary file that says you have ten million dollars. You make the binary file go away. It doesn't go somewhere else, you simply delete the money. Or better yet, the stock market is nothing but electronic records of transactions and ownership. Of course, it is redundantly backed up so if one system fails, three other systems are ready to provide instantaneous service as if there was no interruption. But what if you could destroy all record of ownership of any stock?"

Peter wanted to ask if she could do this, but figured it would be an embarrassingly easy answer. "So you gain access and destroy any record of ownership. If you ever get caught stealing a few thousand dollars from some bank accounts, you do some prison time. If you actually go after the money on the scale you are talking about, the government will never find you. You see, my family has no desire to be in politics. You can have the presidency. We have the money and, if you fuck with the money, they can do anything they want."

"I'd like to try."

☙◊❧

Melissa prepared to drive to the base, telling Peter his computer had been compromised and it would be wise to destroy it and buy a new one.

Lieutenant Gary Barnes was assigned the task of placing discreet cameras above the public access computers. He did not enjoy the order to sit at the monitors watching people come and go. He was not briefed on what they were looking for, just told to look and analyze what he saw.

Melissa entered the darkened room and stood as her eyes adjusted. "I need a live jack."

Lieutenant Barnes pointed to a block of six jacks in the wall. "Pick one."

He was the rare active-duty marine who was also recruited into the NCIS. He was a 0312 and was instrumental in determining the value of the information being passed. He was also ordered to accommodate any request Melissa made. He definitely didn't like the babysitting part.

Melissa booted up as she uncoiled the cable and connected the computer to a jack. She found the correct network and focused her packet sniffer on the two public access computers. "Coffee?"

"You want me to get you coffee, ma'am?" Barnes was not enthused.

"No, I was offering to get you some."

"Sorry, ma'am. Yes, please just black."

Melissa returned and set the coffees down. Two people were working at the computer in the PX. The packets showed nothing more than a restaurant search near the base. Barnes took his eyes away from the monitors to watch the packets. "Ettercap?"

Melissa smiled. "Yes. You know this program."

Barnes shrugged and turned away. They hired a woman to come in and do exactly what he was trained to do. "Yes, ma'am."

Melissa waited for more, but Barnes watched his monitors in silence. "We're looking for someone who might be transferring base secrets to some people in Spain, but they are not Spaniards. If I see some suspicious activity, I am going to have you start the tape and, hopefully, we can identify the person using the computer. Those cameras are pretty good?"

"They can see an ant crawling a mile away. Yes, they are good." His attitude was a little better. "These bad guys, the ones sending the information, what kind of information are they sending?"

"Deployment dates, deployment destinations, training schedules. Pretty serious stuff." Melissa knew how to deny she had given this information out. What she wanted was a reaction. Barnes just nodded his head. "You thinking something?"

"Well, ma'am, it's my job to know who has access to that information. There are just a few people who have access to all of that information at any given time, and they're pretty high up. Security. You say the information is going to one place, but you don't know if more than one person is sending it."

"Correct."

"Okay, so I know three of them are on deployment, and that leaves about fifteen or so people who have access to some of that information who are still on base."

"And you can recognize them by their face?"

"Some. Maybe a third. But that type of information is traded. To know what is going out when is valuable, so they might also be paying someone off or cashing in." Barnes smiled. "That narrows it down to maybe three thousand people or something like that."

"So we sit and watch."

She didn't tell him the patterns she had seen and, by her predictions, she was just a few hours away from seeing more data pass through the system. Barnes passed the time playing a game on line and keeping an eye on the screen when anyone approached. Melissa watched as packets containing deployment locations passed. "Okay, here's a hot one. Record that on the PX computer."

Barnes flicked a switch and watched as a pretty young female marine sat at the computer like anyone else on any given day. He laughed. "Corporal Lindsay Gates. How do you do?"

Melissa flipped open her phone and called Colonel Bartle. "We've got one real time, sir."

Within two minutes there was a knock at the door. Barnes got up to open it and stood at erect attention, saluting.

"At ease, son. She still there?"

"Yes, sir." Barnes closed the on line game, red faced.

"Well, well, Corporal, looks like some time in the brig for you." Colonel Bartle turned to the nervous Lieutenant. "You speak to no one about this. Clear?" The word "clear" cracked like a rifle shot.

"Clear, sir."

CHAPTER 10

The worst part of retirement was when Grady finished his own work for the day and had some time before Sandy and Grady Junior got home. Cable television was nothing more than superficial reality shows and the same hot-air entertainment served up by liberal and conservative pseudo news anchors. These entertainers reminded him of an eighth grade girls' fight. He surfed the channels and stopped when he saw his old boss, Mark Burgess, army colonel, retired. Grady turned the volume up. He wasn't sure of the politics of the cable news host interviewing Mark.

"Colonel Burgess, you had a pretty strong reaction to my first guest. She was fairly adamant the attack on the World Trade Center was planned by us, by our own country. She laid out what she believes is fairly credible evidence—"

"It wasn't evidence. It was bad guessing, at best, and, at worst, it was a slap in the face of every patriotic American," Burgess scowled.

Grady remembered Colonel Burgess well. He took to heart the notion a colonel should be able and willing to do anything he ordered his men to do, only better. He was not a nice guy. He was a warrior who fit best on the battlefield and never did make the transition into civilian life. Grady was surprised they put him in a room alone with someone he didn't agree with. Stupidity was bliss.

"Colonel, let me ask you something." The host leaned back in his chair, placing an index finger to his lips. Mark glared. "You lead a mission into Afghanistan a year prior to the attacks on the World Trade Center," the host continued. "I am somewhat familiar with the rangers and I know that one of your primary targets prior to any attack would be command and control. You go in to destroy telecommunications before an attack, like say before the first Gulf War. Isn't that correct?"

"I can't speak about classified missions, sir."

"I see. Well, let's talk hypothetically here. You are in Afghanistan a year before the attacks on the World Trade Center, you have a team of demolition experts and even one or two telecommunications experts with you. Does that sound plausible?"

"I can't speak about classified missions, sir."

"Right. But you are in a country that is not on anybody's radar on a classified mission as you call it and, a year later, jets smash into the World Trade Center killing thousands of American citizens and then we attack Afghanistan. Do you see how some might see a connection between these two events?"

"I never said I was in Afghanistan on a classified mission. I would not speak publically about any classified mission, sir."

"But, hypothetically, if this was true, don't you see how people will draw conclusions?"

"What conclusions have they drawn?"

"Well, as Ms. Wilkes detailed for us, she heard from a former ranger who was on that mission, who now himself wonders about the coincidence between that mission, the events surrounding the World Trade Center, and our current ongoing war there."

"I heard her suggest a ranger said this. Whoever he is has an active imagination. Let me explain something. Military planners look at the geo-political map every day and think about possible scenarios. If this dictator is overthrown in this country over here, they analyze the security risks to American interests. If they see high quality risks, they plan for that scenario. A classified mission might consist of nothing more than taking a few pictures to give to the CIA. It also might be something more serious than that. I think the planners got this one right. If the politicians did not act soon enough to prevent the attack on the World Trade Center, then shame on them. We did our jobs in the field and we did them well."

Grady noticed Mark leaning forward now. He knew this posture and it was not a good sign.

"Colonel, I have no doubt about your competence. The suggestion that our country manipulated events in order to justify a war in Iraq is a serious issue and we only want to examine—"

"Then you have the wrong guest. You called me and said you wanted to talk about the bravery and valor of the army ranger and I agreed to that. Now you sandbag me into a stupid waste of words over some conspiracy theory being put out there by some woman who should be the Minister of Misinformation for Hugo Chavez." His voice was clear and hard and loud. He stopped speaking and sat back in his chair.

The host was silent, gulping a few times and looking nervously at the camera. "Colonel Burgess, it was a pleasure to speak to a man who is not afraid to speak his mind. We need to go to break and when we come back, we'll ask Colonel Burgess a few more questions about the plane that purportedly struck the Pentagon and then take a look at today's bloopers and snoopers."

Grady muted the volume during the commercials, waiting for Mark to come back on. The plane that struck the Pentagon was one issue that would get Mark fired up. The entertainer's show came back on and Mark was not there. The entertainer looked nervously into the cameras and stammered something about a technical issue and asked to go back to a commercial.

Grady went to his desk and looked up Mark Burgess's number. He dialed and Colonel Burgess answered. "Mark, Grady Marcs here."

"Captain Marcs. Were you watching?"

"Yeah. You did a good job. Why did you leave?"

"I threatened the stupid bastard."

"Geez, you better watch yourself. What ranger are they talking about?"

"Well, I think I know. That sergeant who was shot in the foot and opted out of returning. I think it was him. Hey, I wasn't too hard on the guy, was I?"

Grady could hear the smile coming through the phone. He laughed. "Too hard? Nah. I was just surprised they let you in there alone with him."

"Well, actually they have these bodyguards. Big muscle fairies out of sight of the camera. When I threatened the little weasel, I was hoping one of them would overreact, you know."

"You don't need that kind of publicity. You'd better watch out, or they will end up giving you your own gasbag show."

"I doubt that."

"How's the book coming?"

"Fine. Do you think I'll get back on that show to promote it?"

Grady laughed. "Fat fricking chance. You still planning on coming up to the cabin in Jackson Hole?"

"Yup. See you up there."

Grady thought about the conspiracy theories he had been hearing over the past few years as he dialed Sam's number. The thought that the US planned the whole attack on the World Trade Center was not completely insane to him. The intricacies and the number of people involved were too complex to be simply the job of a nutbag terrorist. So, while he didn't rule out other influences, he stopped himself short of indulging in his own reckless conspiracy theories.

Sam answered on the fourth ring.

"Any activity?" Grady had left access codes for the tracer with Jeffrey.

"No. Nothing. I think, like you said, you scared them off. We should get you in here and settle up like we agreed."

"Nah, I think we should wait another few days and see if they try anything. But I think we can trace these people fairly easily. It's not court room evidence, but I can find out who they are quickly and sic the FBI on them."

"Grady, as much as I want to get these guys, I have to listen to Charles. I have the green light to tighten up security and I want to bring you in on a retainer to help Jeffrey do that, but as for chasing them down, Charles is happy about the insurance coverage, every one of the customers is fully reimbursed and he will not authorize any more expenditures on that, unless they attack again. With Jeffrey monitoring and implementing some of the firewall protection you suggested, I think we can drop it now."

Grady was certain he was listening to the rationale of the next president of Northwest Savings and Loans.

It didn't matter now as Grady Junior walked in the door and wanted to shoot some hoops.

❧❧❧

Grady spent the next morning reading emails about the colonel's performance on television the day before. The reactions were mostly in favor of the old buzzard taking that milk and toast commentator to task. One vet asked if the guy had ever been to war, and the response was overwhelmingly no. The guy's website spoke proudly of his law school days as editor of the law review, his drug days, and his conversion to Christianity having grown up in a family of atheists. Now he lived with his third wife, kids from all three marriages, and was fast becoming a national spokesperson for family values. But as for war, like most cable television superstars, he had not even served in peace. Grady just once wanted to hear commentary about the wars in Afghanistan and Iraq from people who had been on the front lines. Someone once suggested that Grady should put together a proposal for his own show. His only comment was, "It's all about ratings and I would be kicked off after my second show."

He arrived at the bank an hour earlier than Sam had suggested and found his own way to the server room. Jeffrey was busy configuring a new firebox. "Dude, I am so glad you are here. Gene gave me some really mixed up configuration instructions. Knew they came from you, but he got them mixed up. He's got me putting all traffic, even web portal traffic, through the same box, and making sure our customers have access to bill pay and on line accounts, which leaves the ports to fed reporting open as well."

"I thought Charles fired him, I was there. What's he doing now?"

"Theoretically, he is fired, but Charles told me to let him write out instructions, not to have access to the servers. I also changed all the passwords. Also, and I mean, maybe I'm wrong, but I would close the ports we use to data link to the fed until we actually need them again."

Grady smiled. "I like your thinking. Why not use separate access lines and completely separate the two? Keep the web access open twenty-four-seven. The way these guys got in was just because of that kind of architecture. Hide the SAN behind another firewall and allow access to accounts, then at regular intervals update the data bases of all activity. Open a state full session, then shut it down and wait for the next update. In other words, lock it down for once."

Grady suggested trying to penetrate the system regularly, even hiring a company with Charles approval to routinely attempt to break into the system.

Sam appeared at the door. "You two guys free? The board wants to talk to you."

❧❦❧

Grady spent an hour explaining in layman's terms how the system had been compromised. Using a few diagrams on the white board, he succeeded in giving them a primer on networking and network security in a language they completely understood. With this understanding, they were able to see the difference between Gene's configuration and the one Grady attributed to Jeffrey. He showed clearly how there was little change of penetration into the databases unless someone made the mistake of not following proper procedures.

"These guys basically got in because the door was wide open and no one was watching. Now, we know the computer they are using and, if they try again, they will notice some changes. Jeffery has set up what we call a honey pot. They will try to use the old connection if they try again. We will configure a server to look and function like the old configuration, and they will try to move around like they did before. However, this time, they will never find the accounts, let alone have access to them, and we will be gathering information about their computer for the duration of their visit."

"If they do that, what will you do with the information about them?"

"There is nothing I can do without the tacit approval of the board. You tell me what you want me to do. I think what they have done is a crime and if you do not have solid evidence of their past activities, you will have irrefutable evidence going forward. You just say the word."

Sam leaned back in his chair and pursed his lips. "Grady, let's just say that we can always cross that bridge when we get there, or we can turn and go home. You know what I mean? I don't want to rush into anything—"

"San, when you convinced me to take this on, you were the one who wanted prosecution. Now you want me to go along with a deception. I won't do it. You pay me what you think you owe me and we are done, and no you do not have permission to use my trace application. I will uninstall it from your system before I leave here today."

The room was awkwardly silent.

One of the board members shook his head. "Charles, I have not said anything before today. I allowed you to keep Mary and Gene on much longer than I was comfortable with. I mentioned to you last year that, in my limited vision of the IT world, I knew we were vulnerable. In fact, when we were last audited, we got a poor rating for security and I let you sit back and let Mary take the lead. And now, when we have solid knowledge of a person who has been stealing from us, just because we are insured and you do not want public embarrassment, we are just going to sweep this under the carpet like it never existed. I own twenty-five percent of the stock in this bank and you own thirty percent. You remember that as we go forward. I am advising you to seriously reconsider this position."

Grady was already standing and gathering his papers before the man finished. Jeffrey was nervously looking at his hands.

"Mr. Marcs, I will have a check for your services before you leave the building," the board member continued.

Sam was standing now. "Grady, hang on. There are many things to consider here. I'm not saying we're just going to ignore everything. We need to study our options and assess the risk—"

"There is nothing for me to consider here. I have advised you to contact authorities and you have refused. I cannot be a party to this. Jeffrey, can I gain access to your server room to remove my software?" Grady let himself out of the conference room.

☙☙☙

Grady explained to Jeffrey that he never intended to remove the trace software. He showed him several options he had programmed and how to separate what would be useful evidence for the police and what would be useful to Grady. "I have a feeling they might not be back here, but if they are, they will know quickly what we have done and that will probably be the last time. But I want to know as much about them as I can. I just have this feeling they aren't done. You call me whenever you want and, especially, if you see anything. I am also asking you change all of your remote access passwords and delete my account from your system so I have absolutely no access. Could you do that now?"

Jeffrey was quick and efficient. Grady verified his account had been deleted and he no longer had access to the system. The check was waiting for him at the customer service desk as he left.

Grady left the bank and stopped at his favorite bar, the BluWater Bistro, in Leshi, before driving up the hill to the house. The lunch rush was over and a few business people lingered, staring out at the brilliant mild summer day on Lake Washington. Grady wondered why anyone would leave the Pacific Northwest in the summer. Winter, yes, but the summers were the best he had seen anywhere. He ordered a Guinness and observed the slow meticulous care the bartender took to put the proper head on the pint.

What he would do next was something the authorities did not want to know about until it he could warn them of imminent danger. He knew most elected officials and directors of law enforcement depended on others to explain the technicalities of cyber terrorism and did not focus on it much. They spoke of it in broad generalities, one senator even making a fool of himself trying to demonstrate his knowledge of the Internet and how data passed through it. All well and good. Grady understood the process and knew of someone who was capable of breaching a poorly secured bank and stealing in quantities that could be used to finance terrorism. He also had the time and the resources to track them.

CHAPTER 11

Peter decided not to buy another computer. To him, they were just communication devices and he had no appreciation for the complexities of IP addresses, trace route applications, and packet sniffing—whatever they were.

He also thought Melissa was wasting her time. What she had demonstrated was the theft of less than three million dollars. No one account was worth more than ten thousand dollars, and they were insured to one hundred thousand dollars each. At the rate she was going, it would take decades to finally make a dent in the assets of the truly wealthy.

He did call his attorneys and, within a few hours, was given immediate access to ten million dollars in cash. Melissa was impressed, insisting they use the money for computer assets she said she needed. He said he wanted to try something else first, something that would send a clear message.

He had read some letters written by a professional journalist to the families of the Illuminati who had planned to depopulate Asia. Peter considered the article nothing but gibberish. Something like this would never happen. Supposedly the crime gangs in China were sending these families a message through this intermediary— stop your plans to depopulate with disease, starvation, and economic collapse because they knew where these families lived and they would cut them down in their own driveways. This was real action. It was direct, decisive, and significant. If Peter had a pretty good understanding of the banking systems these families used, he knew even better how much they valued their lives and the lives of their children. They believed they were the chosen ones, the elite who were put on this earth to rule, and that made their very lives more sacred than any other living being. They were the ones who decided his sister was worth less than them, really less than all other people, and they removed her from this life as a convenience.

If the Chinese gangs *thought* they knew where they lived, Peter knew exactly where they lived. He had photocopied his grandfather's personal address book and had all of their addresses and notations about when they would most likely be at any one of them. To think there was something like the Illuminati was the preoccupation of the jealous, but to understand just how truly evil most wealthy—really wealthy—people were would drive a normal person to desperate actions.

ɛ·ɔɛ·ɔ

Peter loaded the Ranger Rover and drove north to Malibu. A distant cousin, Gretta, from his father's cousin's family, lived there. She had been a student at Pepperdine and remained on after graduation, her family buying her a Spanish style home in Carbon Mesa near La Costa beach. They had wealth like he did—excessively more than any family needed or even should have. Her father did business with his father. Peter had met her on several occasions, the last time five years earlier in St. Moritz. She would believe his story of being stranded and, knowing her, she would respect his need for privacy and take him in. She would protect one of her own.

He found the street and then the house. It was modest, by her family's standards, no more than four thousand square feet and definitely not the best house in the neighborhood. It was better to be modest and not to flash too much. The houses near her were bigger and there were several expensive cars in the driveways—a statement he had been taught was not necessary to make. The Range Rover was eight years old and would never be noticed next to the Hummers and Rolls Royces.

He knocked on the door and she recognized him immediately. They sat in the kitchen as he explained he was trying to track down a doctor who could write his prescription, but got lost and had been given her address by his lawyers as a safe place to gather himself. She gave him water and offered to make coffee. He thanked her for her kindnesses.

She showed him her portfolio of photography, mostly of the local wildlife threatened by careless development and wild fires. There were several pictures of her hand washing birds after an oil spill.

The view of the ocean was commanding from inside the house, out in the yard, and, especially, from the gazebo at the western edge of the property. They sat in the warm sun, drinking iced tea. She invited him to stay the night and relax and then told the cook to add a guest for dinner.

He slept for a while in the chaise lounge, waking to the warm breeze on his face. The sun was getting close to setting and a few people had gathered in the yard. He stood to join them. These were her friends, school chums, mostly, who shared her vision on protecting endangered species. They drank white wine and ate from the trays set out for them. It appeared to Peter this was a daily occurrence. She introduced him as a friend and he was immediately welcomed in that way cultured and polite people did. They were taught never to introduce each other as family. He had not taken his medication so some wine would be fine and he gratefully accepted a glass.

The tone of the conversation was familiar to him. It was dignified, enlightened, and not vulgar, like the talk of so many newly rich people who struggled to achieve their station. They were young, mostly, no older than thirty-five. These were not the future elected leaders, they were the people with money. People with money were not elected unless they had a personal need to prove themselves. It was these people, his own kind, for whom the laws were written. Not for them to obey, but for their benefit. They never spoke of the politicians, they spoke only of generating the positive energy necessary to move the hearts of the masses.

Dinner was served inside and the table was elegant but not fancy. This was just a weekday dinner party and not a special occasion. She sat in the middle of the table and asked Peter to sit across from her. This way they could hear conversations at both ends as well as talk to each other when they desired. He realized she was a vegan, and it made sense. Saving the animals would not make much sense if she was a carnivore. The food was delightful and her friends were full of praise.

One young man had been drinking too much and began a belligerent monologue about the State of California and the illegal aliens. She looked up at Peter and smiled. The young man had haplessly identified himself as one who had recently come to money. She and Peter listened politely as they had been trained, and when the young man noticed no one else was going to add to his thoughts, he slumped back in his chair and was quiet for the duration of the dinner.

When the dinner was finally over, the guests politely excused themselves. The kitchen help cleaned up behind them as they lingered in the foyer and out into the drive, shaking hands and kissing cheeks.

Peter said good night and went to his room to watch some television. He slept well without the prescriptions. The wine and good food settled him. He woke as the sun peaked in the curtains. He could smell coffee and joined her on the small eastern patio for coffee and some fruit. He set his coffee down and kissed her on the cheek, thanking her for her gracious hospitality. He got into the Ranger Rover, waving as he pulled away from the house. Gretta would be his first.

CHAPTER 12

Lieutenant Barnes enjoyed the view behind the one-way glass. The room was windowless. It stank of urine. The previous prisoner obviously did not like the process or got a clear idea of what the evidence showed. Regardless, it would have been nice to mop the goddam floor. The corporal was handcuffed to the steal table. It did not seem that a pretty lady like her would be a danger, but everyone knew better. A trained marine was a trained marine and a risk of violent behavior all the time. The corporal would not talk. Corporal Gates was tall and steely eyed. They yelled, slammed fists, and threatened her with a one-way trip to Guantanamo, but she said nothing. The civilian NCIS officers had taken over and were now interviewing known associates. They had turned up some lesbian liaisons, an angry former boyfriend who claimed she owed him a thousand dollars, and two collection agencies who were now collecting on her credit cards. The bank records showed several deposits of five thousand dollars over the past two years, totaling over one hundred thousand dollars. Items found in the search of her apartment indicated she was a frequent visitor to the casino on the reservation and the dealers all knew her well. In spite of all the evidence and the potential life sentence, she said nothing to strike a deal.

The naval prosecutor tried to convince her that the longer it took and the more resources were expended in finding the other people involved, the more severe her sentence. Her attorney clarified the laws for her, convincing her to remain silent.

The corporal's response was cold. "Go fuck your dog."

Barnes helped Melissa identify the data types into five distinct categories and she created a rule set in her firebox to monitor for these specific data transfers. The problem was that, even though it was illegal to do so, marines being deployed would often email their destinations to family or participate in online chats or forums about their deployment. Her rules would pick these up, and each one would have to be investigated, even though they would end up being false positives. Lieutenant Barnes was able to quickly sort through most of them and dismiss them for a variety of reasons. What remained was a list of forty-five people NCIS had to interview, five of which were already deployed to Iraq. The work was tedious and Melissa knew they had almost no chance of finding anyone this way.

She knew once the perpetrators saw an arrest, they would either cease the activity, at least for a while, or go under.

"Are there any public libraries or colleges near the campus?"

Barnes nodded. "There's a county library half a mile from the base. You think they would use that?"

"I don't know. I can imagine that, if the library does not require people to create accounts, then all activity is anonymous and the only thing they can monitor is what they see on a screen. And if they have a log in screen, that's easy to boot around."

Barnes thought for a few minutes. "I know something even better than that. Let's go volunteer an afternoon over at the Boys and Girls club. It's right outside the base and we just gave them a computer network last winter."

☙☙☙

The list of active duty marine volunteers was short. There were three—two women and a man. The women always volunteered in the study room. No computers in there. The man, Sergeant Mick Riley, always volunteered in the computer lab. Barnes recognized the name from the list of known associates of Corporal Gates. He had been interviewed and NCIS seemed happy with him. He was scheduled to be in the lab the next morning.

Melissa and Barnes arrived before the scheduled opening and sat in the shift supervisor's office behind a window of one-way glass. She connected her computer to their network and launched her monitoring application. Sergeant Riley arrived at nine, checked in the director's office as required, and spent half an hour shooting pool with the kids. He went into the computer lab when three boys asked him if they could do research on the Internet. He logged them in with the generic guest account and then himself onto another computer. He launched an email application and started to compose an email. One boy asked for his help and Riley got up and spent ten minutes helping him.

Melissa smiled, pointing at the screen. She had been able to capture the screen shot of his email. The content was a list of twenty marines who were being transferred from one base in Iraq on temporary assignment to another, including the dates of travel. Sergeant Riley went back to his email and stayed with the boys in the computer lab until the NCIS and the local police arrived to arrest him. It was over by lunchtime.

える

Barnes had suggested the beer. Melissa was a civilian and there were no rules against that. "Is it always so easy?" he asked.

"Not with the really smart ones, but those are few and far between. Most people are really stupid when it comes to computers. I mean sending classified troop movement information in an email. I guess it is so simplistic some investigators might not even look there."

He asked what motivated her. She thought for a moment. She could never tell this lieutenant her real motivation. He was trained to draw conclusions and project seemingly unrelated bits of information into possible threats. If she told him her father had worked for a defense contractor for more than twenty years after serving in Vietnam and he was laid off from his management position when they discovered he had cancer, Barnes would have been compassionate, but he would never forget what she said. If she went on to tell him they terminated his health care and, after selling the house and eating through his retirement, it all ran out and he died. Barnes would laugh at the short sightedness of the military and the corporate world, but he would also begin to create a profile of her in his mind. He would conclude she was capable of doing something to retaliate against the corporation who was earning millions from defense contracts and disposing of human capital at the earliest sign of inconvenience.

She told him she had dated an army captain for a while. He had been killed in a training accident and this was all the motivation she needed. She worked as a civilian contractor to the military in his loving memory.

The conversation halted. They both knew they were trying to mine brain data and they both knew it was worth the effort.

"I'm being deployed to the poppy fields to help the current corrupt version of government in Afghanistan sell drugs to the west. And have my ass shot at. Good luck on your little investigation while I 'defend' my country." The lieutenant used his fingers to air-quote defend.

"Do your job and man up." She thanked Barnes for the beer and went home.

CHAPTER 13

It was nice to finally have Grady Junior out of school. They could now leave on vacation for the next four weeks, right through the Fourth of July weekend. This was often the best times to leave Seattle, since the sun really didn't come out there much until after the fourth. Grady had arranged with Jeffery to communicate to him any suspicious activity and he would also monitor the computer that had been used for the last theft. For him, life could become one big vacation and he knew that would bore him. A little work, now and then, served to occupy his mind and allowed him to hold more cash reserves in his investment portfolio.

Sandy had arranged for the board of directors of her foundation to meet for the week prior to the fourth so she would also be spending time revising the vision statement and business plan intended to drive the foundation for the next five years. She had finished her doctorate in Economics before founding the company with Grady and, after they sold, was in a position to undertake her favorite research through the foundation. Her focus was to examine the effects the Internet has on the economic development of extremely poor countries. Her life was one of productive daily work, and a little vacation, now and then, helped her refocus.

Grady Junior was anxious to get a chance to sleep in and do some fishing. He could still remember the years when his father was away at war. There was no money for a vacation and he spent his summers helping his mother in the company office. This was much better.

Grady had prepared the cabin for the vacation when he met Sam there in early for the weekend in May. The property management company, who rented the cabin out when they were not using it, charged extra to unpack and repack their personal belongings. This gave Grady an excuse to go ahead of the family and get some late spring fishing and climbing in. He was close to convincing Sandy to move to Jackson Hole permanently with the promise they would sell the Seattle house and buy something bigger in Jackson Hole. He had even mentioned the idea of shopping around during this vacation. After a leisurely two-day drive, they arrived in time to sit down to dinner.

Colonel Mark Burgess arrived the next afternoon with his family—his second wife Martha and her son Derrick, who was a year younger than Grady Junior. They would occupy the two guest rooms. They walked into town and ate dinner, afterward sitting in the living room catching up. The women went to a wine bar Grady detested and he told Mark he had some beer at the cabin. The boys went upstairs to watch a movie.

They didn't like talking about the war days. It wasn't worth it. But the colonel had a few letters he had received after his appearance on the cable network talk show. What he found most shocking was the variety of conspiracy theories. He read the most disturbing one out loud.

"Colonel Burgess, you are nothing more than a dupe

and a clown. Your role in the death of five thousand innocent people in the World Trade Center is, at best, immoral, if not outright sinful. You are a party to the intentional destruction of the American way of life. You have overseen operations that serve to do nothing but destroy our freedoms and piss on the Constitution of the United States. You knew full well when you went into Afghanistan that we were going to intentionally attack the WTC ourselves and cause these endless wars that will serve no other purpose but to drain our economy and leave us vulnerable to economic collapse. Find the manhood to admit your role in this and repudiate all you have done before we witness the fall of the United States of America."

The colonel paused when he was finished and then folded the letter. "The worst part is I confirmed it was Sergeant Willis who revealed our names and gave them details of the missions. He's going to get a visit here shortly."

"Mark, we've been dealing with this crap since 9/11. Forget about it. I warned you not to do this sort of thing." Grady offered him another beer and he accepted.

"What's this thing you're working on up there in Seattle?"

Grady yelled from the kitchen, "Someone's pilfering small amounts of money from a large number of bank accounts."

"That should be an easy catch."

"Should be, yes, but the bank pulled the plug on the investigation and refuses to go forward with prosecution. I have all the intel I need to track the guy, and I am going to keep tabs on him."

"Joy ride or terrorists?"

"I don't know. Once I track them for a while, I'll know where the money is going."

"I thought they tracked everything now, even your

debit card purchases. Wasn't that governor who was caught flinging it with that whore trying to evade detection?"

"They detect what they want to detect. If they said they were looking for money transfers to track terrorists, that's probably not true. They were tracking *his* money activity to catch *him*, and they did."

Burgess laughed. "Yeah, he made enough enemies, someone was bound to go after him."

"I have a hunch, though, that I am not seeing everything in this bank deal. I've tracked activity like this before and usually there is an identifiable mark, a calling card if you will. People approach technology with different problem-solving skills and that is reflected in the type of viruses, trojans, or hacking techniques they use. This was pretty good. I have a guy on the inside there who is scouring the servers, looking for any scripts this guy may have left behind."

"Well, you know me. I am an old POTS guy. Put up a wooden pole, put some glass insulators on it, string some wire, and you have a phone system. I'm too old for the new stuff." Burgess looked around and lowered his tone. "Maybe you can help me. I'm not huge on computers, but Derrick has been acting strange lately, so much time on the computer. I don't know how to track what he's doing."

Grady didn't smile. "Did he bring it with him?"

"No, it's a desk top job."

"What do you think is going on?"

"He says he met some new friends on line. Martha told him to print out all the chats he has, but I don't think he's doing that. I'm a little worried."

"When you get home, I will send you a program I want you to put on his computer and I am going to set up a monitoring system that will show you exactly what he is doing any time you want to see." Grady sipped his beer. "Be careful here, Mark, this could be completely innocent or really terrible. I wouldn't tell Martha about it until you can figure out what's going on."

❧❧❧

The ladies returned with six bottles of very good wine for the kitchen. Grady admired their choices. He loved good wine with dinner. He just hated pretentious wine bars full of money sharks and lawyers. They chatted until it was late and promised to get up early for some fishing. Burgess and Grady would be up at five and they knew the ladies would sleep until nine, the boys probably until ten. They also knew this was just the way they liked it.

Grady had an email from Jeffrey. He had found a script running on the authentication server that copied every user name and password entered into an ATM machine. Grady opened the script in an editor and read the code. It was a very simple Java script, but with very serious consequences. The only way it could have been installed was with administrative access. He thought for a moment again about Gene Surrey, wondering if he could have given someone access, but the dismissed the idea. He was an idiot and wouldn't know what he was looking at.

CHAPTER 14

Melissa called it the "Bankers Delight." It was just a little code—a short script that barely needed standard commentary to tell an individual what it was. It wasn't like one of those smash and dash things the crackers put together to destroy data. She wanted to preserve the data, to share it with the owner. It worked like a virtual camera. When a banking customer went to an ATM, they slid their card through the magnetic reader and were required only to enter a four-digit security code. All she wanted was the account number and that four-digit code. Well…then the money, after that.

Peter did not like her condescending tone when she was explaining technical concepts. He fidgeted as she tried to over simplify the process. He wanted to know how the script was put into place. She explained this by demonstrating how she had selected and then gained access to Northwest Bank and Trust.

She had purchased a vendor's table at a security conference in San Francisco. She crafted her brochures to specifically target small, locally owned banks who had minimal information systems personnel, and who usually had no real security plan in place, other than a few out-of-the-box monitoring solutions. Her services ranged from risk assessments right through complete security plan development and implementation.

On the surface, she would secure the systems. They got what they paid for. Knowing these network administrators were usually very smart but understaffed and not fully funded, she gave them many free tools and a lot of free advice over and above the contracted security services. She always won their confidence, especially, when—dressed to win over hearts of lonely men—she invited the administrators out for drinks after one or two arduous days in the server room. These would usually end with a well-planned call on her cell phone, usually nothing more than an automatic reminder call she set up on her own computer. She would pretend it was a crucial incident at another bank and leave before the evening got too festive. The next day she would typically have full administrative access and would, therefore, have the ability to install her script, which had a fifteen-week delay. The client bank would experience superior security results and she would win another industry referral.

At the San Francisco conference, a short man, smelling of Old Spice and dressed in a blue polyester shirt with a white penholder in the shirt pocket, had stopped by the booth. He'd introduced himself as Gene Surrey, Chief Security Officer of Northwest Bank and Trust. His business card said Network Administrator, but the title of CSO always slipped into every subsequent conversation he had with her. She used the title liberally and he seemed to like that.

At first, he was like every other administrator from a small bank. He flat out told her he had things covered and he was burning time on the display floor until the next session. She knew most of these administrators were on a very small per diem for food and often hung around vendor booths talking up their successes in hopes of a complimentary meal. It was just after noon and the display floor was mostly vacant. The offer for lunch from a tall, beautiful woman was rarely refused but, in this case, Gene Surrey was so eager she almost regretted asking him. The mean, tight grin on his face bothered her.

She chose a table close to the cashier. She caught her eye and winked as Gene sat heavily and ordered a double scotch. During the course of the lunch, he drank three doubles and ate the most expensive steak and shrimp offering on the menu. She knew he was calculating that he could use his lunch and dinner per diem for dinner now and live large on the trip.

She tried to steer the conversation toward details about his systems and he steered it right back to his ex-wife, their two children living in Los Angeles with her, and how lonely Seattle could be during the winter. She finally got him to talk about his security by stroking his ego about how small banks never allocated enough money for adequate security, and the one horse show was supposed to do all things. She slipped in how her services could often be so specific and targeted, they could be paid for over time through small line items and no one would even know she had been hired. All the work was done remotely and only with the administrators approval and knowledge. He would be in total control and she would simply be a helping hand. He raised his eyebrows when she said that.

He took her card and promised to call. She met two other network administrators—one later that day when the display floor was closing. He straggled along as security approached him twice, reminding him the display would reopen at eight o'clock the next morning. She had been invited to a hosted hospitality bar on the upper deck of the hotel, where the pool and Jacuzzi were located. She could bring a guest. He appeared to be in his late twenties, fairly good looking, but with the classic shyness of a highly intelligent technical person. He also appeared to be underfunded and even dangerously malnourished. He introduced himself as the network administrator for a credit union in Montana. She wondered if he might want to join her at the hospitality bar. He laughed and said, yes, of course.

This mark was a little easier. He had discretionary funds for outsourcing consulting services and had been directed to find someone to conduct a security risk assessment. This told her they were aware of security issues and this would have to take more time. She would win the contract, no doubt, but the time frame for implementing her script would be prolonged by as much as three to four months.

Once she was certain of the contract, she took her emergency call and left him with the hardware vendors who had hosted the bar. He was their problem now.

Gene Surrey did call two days after the conference and asked her to fly to Seattle and start a risk assessment. He had found her retainer and five weeks of consulting fees in three line items he rarely used. She agreed to invoice him for three different types of software instead of consulting services.

Following the initial consultation in Seattle, she gained full administrative remote access and began the work of securing his network. She actually did nothing to secure the network and, after using up only two weeks of his funds, declared the system safe and actually refunded some of the money directly to him. She told him she would invoice him for two more weeks and just send him the money. Gene laughed that mean little laugh over the phone, thanking her and offering to show her a good time

in Seattle. She declined. Fifteen weeks later, on a quiet
Sunday morning, she accessed the accounts and took the
money. This continued until she knew she had been detected, on Peter's computer. Now it was time to pay a visit to Montana.

Peter was intrigued, but not convinced yet this would
have much of an impact. How did she intend to use this
system of hers, say on the New York Stock Exchange?
She asked him how many people he personally knew
there and he said a few. She asked how many his father
knew and he said everyone and most of them owed him
money. She admitted the system would need to be dra-
matically more sophisticated, but the essential truth was
the most vulnerable point in any computer network was
the people who managed them. He didn't quite grasp this,
but was willing to talk further. In the meantime, he was
going to show her what impact a direct hit would have.

Peter explained the young woman was a member of
one of the families often referred to as the original thirteen bloodlines, granddaughter to one of the wealthiest
industrialists in Europe who also now owned several oil
fields in Russia. They were wealthy before the two world
wars but, after, the wealth became obscene by any standard. They stopped counting exactly how much they were
worth, although they had a good idea. The patriarch, now
eighty years old, had been a voluntary member of the Hitler Youth and had recruited a young man who would later
become the religious leader of the Roman Catholic
Church.

The pope had long ago disavowed his forced partici-
pation in the Hitler Youth, distancing himself in every
way from the nature and intent of the group, but the
grandfather had not. He relished the days. While he ended up married, with five healthy sons, he loved frolicking
nude with the other Hitler Youth, thinking nothing of the

homosexual implications. It was a powerfully perverted time and he spoke often of it with great fondness. If any of his family expressed discomfort with this history, he disowned them.

His summer estate was a thirty-acre walled encampment that was more nudist colony than summer home. If you were family, you went every summer without question. If you refused, you never saw another dime. Peter recalled being sent there when he was fourteen and refusing to undress. He was sent home immediately and the grandfather apologized to Peter's grandfather for any embarrassment.

The idea of depopulating certain races or nations was something the grandfather invested much time and money studying. He hosted very tightly guarded and private discussion groups with like-minded people. The fact that no one outside of this circle of fifteen or twenty people had ever heard about it was a testament to the control the old man had on the people around him.

"But why kill his granddaughter?"

"Because it will hurt him more than anyone else."

Melissa refused to go along. "I don't how what this old man does in the nude has to do with killing his granddaughter. Did he kill your sister? Why not kill your father or your grandfather?"

"I just might." Peter laughed coyly. "The whole bunch of them should be killed. They are two generations of the most heinous men in history, and most of the women, too."

⋐⋙⋐⋙

An hour after Peter drove away, Melissa booted his laptop in the motorhome and began to explore some options. After two hours of pinging known IP addresses, she found one of the mainframes for the NASDAQ. It wasn't the New York Stock Exchange, but it would do for preliminary research.

She quickly discovered the honey pot, a virtual area within the network that appeared to be an unsecured server containing some real information. It was designed to give a cracker the false impression they were into the server, while the security personnel acquired information about the computer the cracker was using. She left before any data was accessed, read, or altered. She would not go unnoticed, but they would not come after her. She had accessed an area anyone with a computer would have also been able to get into and she had done nothing. After two more hours of exchanging information with other anonymous crackers, she was able to locate the lock box for the New York Stock Exchange. She knew better than to execute any kind of exploit. She would, no doubt, be detected and monitored. There was a better way

∞∞∞

Peter arrived three hours later in front of the house in Carbon Mesa. Gretta was home working on her environmental cause. She was expecting a few people from the organization later for dinner and he was welcome to stay. He thought that would be a good idea and said he would think about it, but first he wanted to talk. Did she have the time? She did, just later. She told him to relax, get something from the kitchen, and she would be around.

The afternoon sun filtered through the leaded-glass windows in the front door. The decor was old Europe. Peter wasn't sure why that surprised him. The kitchen was also dated, but nicely appointed. His eyes caught the full complement of copper pots and pans, lined up exactly to size.

A short Mexican woman smiled at him and said welcome. She motioned to the refrigerator. "You want something?"

"Just a light lunch, maybe a sandwich and some iced tea."

Iced tea and small sandwiches were served outside on the warm breezy patio. He felt odd and wanted to understand what he was feeling before he did anything. The sandwiches were good. Maybe he was just hungry. Gretta found him on the patio an hour later and sat next to him.

"What would you do without all of this?"

"What do you mean?"

"What if, all of a sudden, our parents and grandparents lost everything?"

She laughed. "Oh, you. You, better than anyone, know that isn't going to happen. I mean the world would have to come to an end before that would happen. If we die, everyone would also be dead."

"I'm not so sure of that."

"Now, stop this. You used to do this when you were, like, twelve. We're not going to die. No one is going to creep up in the dark and kill us."

"You seem very confident. You don't think our families have inflicted enough harm that some group might be motivated to fight back? Your grandfather always talks about getting rid of the chinks and the gooks. Does he really believe that he can do that, or is he just a racist Nazi holdover from the war?"

She looked at him for a few minutes in silence. "My grandfather will be dead in a few years, five at the most. He rants on and on about these things and no one takes him seriously. I mean, it is virtually impossible to actually do what he rambles on about. He's a demented old man who does not have a clear grasp of reality. You simply cannot annihilate billions of people. We laugh behind his back."

"You also don't challenge him."

"Peter, grandfather is still sharp enough to cut people out of the will. We humor him. I feel sorry for the people he hates so much, but they are never around when he talks like that. He only mentions it to family now. I know he used to talk to people, other people like us, about it, but no one ever took him seriously."

"The Chinese do. They have gangs and they're going to come after anyone who talks like that. You know they believe the SARS virus was actually an attempt to put this thinking into action."

Gretta wondered how many of their families would also suffer mental disorders. "Peter, I am not afraid of the Chinese. We do business with them and have been for centuries. They do not want to see us die. If any one of them has ever heard my grandfather talk this way, and I doubt they have, they would know instantly it is not possible for him to effect this in any way." She stood when the lunch plates were cleared away. "If you want to take a nap or something, I have some more work I want to get done."

"Yes, I think that would be good"

❦❦❦

Gretta called her father's office and left a message with his personal secretary to call her. She wanted to talk to someone about Peter, maybe get back to his family. She took three calls and the importance of her concern for him diminished.

CHAPTER 15

The information cost Melissa a modified copy of the program she used on Northwest Bank and Trust, but it was far more valuable. She was looking at the logical diagram of the network used every day to record the sale and purchase of stocks. It was not as elaborate as she had suspected it might be. It was actually brilliant in its simplicity. It was far easier to protect this architecture than something more complicated. It was well protected from outside penetration. No one except the most serious crackers would try an external exploit and, given what she saw, they would be easily detected.

What she did see were internal opportunities. The protection of the electronic financial infrastructure that drove the American economy was always a serious consideration at Homeland Security. Lieutenant Barnes would be helpful. Through him, she could get an introduction by finding some evidence of attempted cracking of the system. She already had a reputation upstream from him and she would get access.

She created a profile of a male cracker on a rant site focusing on hatred for the Masons. She called herself

"SatanInsideYou." Using Peter's computer, she contributed several postings and set out to voraciously insult any member who tried to debunk the notion the Masons were out to destroy the United States of America.

It didn't take long to find a few like-minded crackers on these sites. These were people all too willing to spend their nights ranting and raving about the evils of the world, juiced up on energy drinks, and swapping viruses and trojans. With little provocation, they would gladly try to crack any system.

She narrowed her focus on two members who bragged about trying to crack the Department of Defense. They didn't get in. She offered the diagram for the New York Stock Exchange computer systems. They bit and for three more hours they set out a plan to crack the system externally. She offered her own version of a multiplatform password crack and they liked it. In exchange, she got their versions of a kill virus, intended to destroy data. They set a time intended to effect maximum damage—at the closing bell in two days. She told them it was a significant anniversary and they believed her.

She used people like this often—maladjusted males, mostly, who would provide her with a reason for some entity to hire her expertise to find the perpetrators. They would stomp around the perimeter and she would get hired in to stop them. She became the trusted hero and, sometimes, the perpetrators would actually be prosecuted.

At seven in the morning, she knew Lieutenant Barnes would have already been at his desk for half an hour. His secretary put her through and he took the call. He listened and then gave her two numbers, one of which was a direct line to the Directorate of Science and Technology. The associate director of that department had served with him in the first Gulf War. Barnes offered to call him first, and then called her back ten minutes later to tell her the associate director was expecting her call.

She understood this was a former marine, who knew his job of defeating a retreating enemy well, but he knew nothing of computer systems. He took in what he could and told her he would introduce her directly to a contact he had who investigated cyber threats. Could she fly out to New York? She could. Tomorrow? Yes. A ticket would be waiting for her when she checked in. She was to find Brett Douglass and he would be her primary contact.

It was that easy. She called Lieutenant Barnes back and he thanked her for her vigilant service to the United States of America. He added something like, it was patriots like her who would ensure the survival of this great nation forever.

She could barely contain her laugh.

☙❧

Melissa slept for a few hours, woken by Peter as he slammed the front door and locked it.

"Melissa, are you home?"

She appeared in the hallway. "I got in. I am going to get into the New York Stock Exchange." She could see Peter was not listening. His eyes were glazed over.

"What did you say?"

"The New York Stock Exchange. I'm in. I fly out there tomorrow. New York."

Peter hesitated. "Oh, yeah? Wow."

"I need you to come along. I need as much access as I can get." He was still not listening. "What's the matter?"

"I did it. This morning, really early, I went in and I killed her." Peter sat on the sofa. "It was so much easier than I ever thought it would be."

"You killed that young woman you told me about?"

"Yes." Peter was smiling. "My cousin Gretta."

"Where is she?"

"In her bed. She is still in her bed."

Melissa bit her knuckle. "Oh, shit. This ruins everything. People saw your Range Rover there. They'll be looking for it and my neighbors have seen one around, yours. They will report it."

"I left it there. It's registered to someone who has been dead for ten years, someone who also knew her. I just thought of that this morning. And she died from drugs. I gave her drugs. A lot of them. She was pretty drunk still and she just took them down. I think it looks like a suicide."

Melissa looked out the front window at the late model Lexus parked in the driveway. "Do I want to know who that belongs to?"

"I used an assumed name my father's attorneys gave me. I've never done that before, but it went right through. I just called the lawyers and the car dealer had money right away. It's a pretty slick car." He sat forward. "I need your help. I have a plan."

"This is murder."

"I know and I will, in time, admit to it. Now, I think it is best to tell you. Legally, I am mentally disabled. So the doctors say. I take these drugs and when I don't, I am legally not accountable, so I didn't take my drugs and I killed her. But first I need your help. I want my family to think someone is coming after them."

"Then I need you in New York. You need to fly with me tomorrow."

"Why tomorrow?"

"There will be a ticket waiting for me—"

"No, that won't work. I will call the attorneys and they will have a private jet ready for us in a couple of hours. I have an apartment on Park Avenue and we will stay there. I will introduce you to my father and grandfather. They will be delighted." He sat back on the sofa. "That is until they hear what I have to tell them."

She felt odd about his new tone of voice. Melissa rubbed his shoulder and he smiled. "How did it feel, you know..."

"Powerful. I felt very powerful."

CHAPTER 16

After the war, the family had changed their surname. After many decades of industrious work and accumulation of massive wealth, their association with the horrors of Hitler's Whermacht haunted them. The family elders changed their surname and forbid any heir to use the original family name in public ever again. In spite of this, they would always know who they really were and would use their proper surname in private. They took the name Schultz instead. They adopted the Schultz family crest and had the name and crest carved into the stone archway over the gate to the summer estate.

The summer estate was located within view of the North Sea outside of the small town of Sankt Peter-Ording, covering almost three hundred acres and holding five small to medium sized lakes. It was conveniently situated just over a hundred miles from the family estate in Hamburg. There were enough buildings to hold the entire extended family and numerous guests. In spite of the frigid winters, the staff lived on the estate year round. In the summer, the hot July and August days on the North Sea provided the perfect private summer vacation. The main entrance, and the only road onto the fenced land, was guarded continuously.

For that reason, the estate was frequently visited by wealthy, powerful, and royal families across Europe and the United States. The Schultz family, even before assuming this surname, had made it a point never to invite a non-Caucasian person onto the property in the three hundred years they had owned it.

The main lodge was a quarter mile from the entrance. There were rooms for twenty-five family members or guests on the first, second, and third levels and two modest dormitories for the staff in the basement. Ten smaller lodges were scattered around the lakes and several small cabanas dotted the private beach front.

During this first week of summer vacation, only the Schultz family and a few friends of the children were in residence.

It had been a day of great summer fun around the pool. It was a hot day and the mandatory nudity was not unwelcome. It was, in fact, so commonplace that no one ever gave it a thought anymore—not even the guests who simply did as their hosts did.

They gathered, clothed, around the common dining room. The headcount revealed thirty-five dinner guests. Instead of formal table service, a buffet was standard, which allowed them to eat and talk casually. This was unlike meal times in their city mansions, where these events were very formal and highly structured.

The black Mercedes Benz rolled quietly through the thick forest bordering the estate and stopped at the gate. Because of the winding nature of the road and the dense foliage, it took several minutes to get to the gate from the main road. An armed guard recognized the car, but routinely asked for identification. Ernst was a family attorney and a frequent visitor during the summer holidays so the family could continue to conduct business while away from their offices.

Ernst waited in the foyer of the lodge. He was announced and invited to join the group for supper. He declined, indicating his business was serious and he needed to speak to the elder Schultz.

Armand Schultz motioned for his four sons to join him and they gathered in a study off the library. The five, as the family called them, made all of the decisions for the family.

Ernst laid the photographs of Gretta out carefully and silently. No one spoke. It was obvious she had died without a struggle and the photographs of the empty pill bottles suggested suicide.

He allowed them some time to reflect on the reality of losing one of their own. "We have some options."

Armand Schultz stood and waved his hand. "Keep this out of the press, make no mention of it. Do you understand, Ernst? I don't want this on the front page of the Los Angeles Times. This is our matter and we will handle it. Bring her home immediately and we will arrange to bury her here. I want her home. You have not told them, correct?" Ernst nodded. Armand looked around the room at his four sons. "Speak to no one about this." He waved his arm toward the dining room and turned to the eldest son. "Klaus, you stay here. You three, go back in there and act as if nothing has happened. Ernst, you stay here."

Armand sat quietly and stared out the window. "Klaus, this is your daughter. I will respect any reaction you might have, but I want to help you think through this before you decide what to do. Don't let your emotions over ride what should be a clear, effective response." Klaus nodded. Armand turned to another son. "Ernst, this was made to look like a suicide, but is there something we do not know? Have the police been notified?"

Ernst shook his head. "No police. Your lawyers in Los Angeles were notified by the maid when she discovered Gretta. Her body is currently being preserved at a private mortuary awaiting your instructions."

Armand sat quietly for a moment. "Send the forensics lab over there and tell them to give the results directly to me." Ernest nodded and left quietly. Armand sighed. "I will call the priest."

❦

It was just after the routine weekday Mass that the priest in Mulege took the call on his small, vibrating phone. He had just locked the small safe and hid the key. He leaned back against the cabinetry holding the sacred vestments and listened. His hand brushed through his hair several times and he sighed deeply, groaning occasionally. He only said yes fifteen or twenty times, acknowledging that he understood and agreed to whatever was being spoken on the other end. The call ended and he sat staring out the window. He dialed a number and waited for an answer. "Martin, I need to get to the compound in Germany and I need to leave today...Yes, though Mexico City...Yes, it is always first class."

CHAPTER 17

G rady rappelled down the rock face upside down, flipping over just in time to land on his feet. Onlookers either cheered or yelled at him, calling him a show off. Burgess followed close behind, using the same technique.

"Now it's your turn." Grady slapped the rope against the rock face. "Put that safety rope on Derrick, and then you come after him." He knew his son would never express any of the fear he was feeling. He would just do as he was told and hope it turned out. Derrick rappelled feet first. Grady Junior lowered the backpack for the gear to the base of the rock, flipped over head first, and rappelled to the ground. His landing was not as smooth as his father's, but it was clean and safe.

Other climbers now walked by and commented on how they knew this method was common in the military. They usually asked what branch and nodded respectfully when they heard it was the rangers.

If the conversation ever drifted toward war stories, both Grady and Burgess would change the subject. This was something the whole company had agreed on. They would never reveal the details of any mission, secret or not, and they would never talk about the human beings who lost their lives in what had been determined to be proper by the rules of engagement. They had a distinct distaste for the blowhards who bragged about their kills. This was not honorable warfare. They hated, even more, the civilians, who, upon learning of their military experience, would always ask if they had killed anyone. This question was always ignored and, if the person persisted, they were flatly told never to ask the question again.

This did not diminish their ability to kill. While investigating an FBI special agent, Grady discovered he had been routinely stealing classified information from defense contractor information systems and selling these secrets to the Chinese. There was confusion in the communications surrounding the arrest of the agent, and Grady was trapped alone with him in a locked server room. The agent pulled his gun and fully intended to kill Grady, but Grady pulled the knife he carried strapped to his leg and won. The room was sanitized and the incident was declared self-defense. While he hoped he would never have to use it again, he always carried the knife whenever he could legally do so.

Jackson Hole, Wyoming, was a place he figured he would probably never need the knife, but it was always there, strapped to his left leg. While other tourists wandered the streets of this luxurious resort town with beer guts and ugly shorts, no matter the temperature, he wore long pants, even while rock climbing. The only exception was that during a long hike to the higher lakes with Mark and the boys, he always instigated the quick skinny dip to cool off. These didn't last long as the lakes were usually at the dripping end of a snow field and extremely cold.

In the afternoons, Burgess settled down to his laptop on the front porch table to work on his book. The boys were off to town on their bikes and Grady went to his office to work. They had converted the garage to a working office so he and Sandy could get something accomplished even on their vacations. Sandy was invariably in the office long before Grady finished with his morning fun.

Sandy was busy preparing for her board meeting. Martha was doing footwork at the hotel where the other members of the board were going to meet. "If I didn't have her, I'd be lost. You boys can just run around doing blood sport things, we have work."

Grady knew better than to get in her way or disturb her. He focused on analyzing the code Jeffrey had sent. If it was complex code with detailed comments, he could usually trace the school or source where the person had learned to program. Mostly, however, people just left telltale marks in the code, such as their nickname or comments about their children. The most elaborate mark was left by an electronics engineer who had built custom motherboards. He could solder a likeness of his cat on the board, complete with the patch over his eye. Crackers were narcissists and wanted you to know they got in. But if the code was so simple there was no room for comments, it was often the destination of the data, if any, that would give it away. Short of that, often the only way to determine the source of the code was to plant it on a computer, run it, and see what happened.

There was a line of code that ran a remote application called "Bankers Delight." He opened a monitoring application and ran the code. He first saw the program scan his program files and registry and it discovered data from a test banking session he and Jeffrey had run. It parsed out everything except the name on the account, the account number, and routing number of the bank. He guessed the remote call was going to find the bank associated with the routing number and he was right. The program accessed a database and identified the routing number as Northwest Bank and Trust. He was prompted to enter the default gateway. He guessed he could ping the bank's name and see what came up, but if there was any kind of perimeter monitoring, he would be detected. He called Jeffrey to tell him he was going to trip the monitoring device and to reset the system to the configurations Gene had established.

Jeffrey sat at his console, watching. Grady entered the default gateway and the remote application immediately scanned for passwords associated with the account. It took less than five seconds to produce the password and the account owner's social security number. Grady was prompted to enter the name on the account, then the password, and then the social security number associated with the account with the same password. He was in.

He called Jeffery again. "For this program to work, it was an inside job. Someone had to get your default gateway and I doubt I could see that no matter how inept Gene Surrey was."

"You mean like an outside contractor."

"Yep."

"Well, I've been tasked with auditing some of Gene's expense reports, along with accounting, and we discovered some payouts to a consultant run through some rarely used accounts."

"When did he make the payments?"

"Well, it looks like maybe eight weeks ago it started. Way long before the money started disappearing."

Grady smiled and shook his head. "Jeffrey, we're dealing with a very smart person. Whoever it is gains access or plants the code through an inside contact and it has a time bomb on it that is deleted upon activation. That's just my educated guess." He went back to the database of routing numbers. "What scares me the most is the number of checking account routing numbers in this database and it looks like a lot of them have access to the account numbers associated with those routing numbers. This is not good."

He guessed there were almost four hundred different banks in the data base. Once the routing number was run, the program called up all account numbers and cracked the passwords. "Jeffrey, do you keep your money in the bank or are you one of those guys who stuffs hundred dollar bills into his mattress?"

"Direct deposit and I use my bank card for everything."

"Then you say nothing about this. You know our banking system only works if people believe it's secure. The second they know how extensive this is, it's over."

CHAPTER 18

New York in June was usually not terrible, but this June was an exception. The heat wave had started right after Memorial Day and was getting worse. When Melissa stood on the sidewalk, she felt her clothes clinging to her skin. She found it difficult to breathe. Peter paid the driver and pointed at the revolving door on the side of the building. The man in the funny suit collected their bags and followed them.

"Sir, it's so nice to see you back in New York. It's been too long." He stepped ahead of them and pressed the button for the elevator. "Would you like me to take these up with you?"

"No, thanks, John." Peter handed him a twenty dollar bill.

There were only four options on the elevator panel—the garage, floors one, sixteen, and seventeen. Peter noticed Melissa's puzzled look. "We own the building. My father keeps an apartment on the top floor and I live on the sixteenth when I am in New York."

"And the rest of the building?"

"Offices for my father's attorneys." Peter smiled.

"They enter from the garage. We usually never see them, just talk on the phone. If they need to give us anything, they just leave it with John"

She guessed the apartment was more than three-thousand square feet. There were three master suites and four bedrooms. It was not what she would call plush, just well appointed. She recognized works of various well-known artists and, from her little exposure to art history, surmised many of them were originals. They entered the kitchen and, instead of a gaudy stainless restaurant-looking facility, it was a really nice kitchen, done in what she knew, but could never afford—a modern Italian design. Peter pressed a button in the kitchen and a maid appeared.

She wore the traditional black and white uniform "Hello, sir, can I fix you something to eat?"

"I think we can manage, thank you. You have some turkey in the refrigerator for sandwiches?" he nodded and left.

Peter answered his phone. He spoke quietly for a few moments and hung up. "That was my father. John is required to call him whenever I arrive." He was quiet as he showed Melissa to his bedroom suite. "Unless you object, I think I will be easier for us if we…uhm…just say, like, we're together. If that bothers you—"

"No, that's fine. Thanks for the heads up. I need a computer."

He showed her a desk top in the office.

"I need one they can't trace to you."

He said he could have had one sent for free, but she insisted they buy one. She suggested looking for one on the Internet from a library or someplace where there were anonymous users. There was a quiet ringing from one of the other rooms. Peter stopped and raised his eyebrows.

"Well, here we go. My father is on his way down."

Melissa had met what she considered wealthy people—one of them owned the car dealership in her hometown and was the only other family that owned a swimming pool other than the doctor and the town lawyer. She hesitated, somewhat in awe, as the tall gray-haired man casually strolled through the living room.

The father stopped and took a hard, quick look at her and his face melted into a warm smile. "Son, so good to see you. Who, may I ask, is your friend?" He held out both hands to grasp hers.

"Father, this is Melissa, the reason I came home. I wanted you to meet her."

"Indeed. Young lady, you are too good looking for my son, I want you to know that. Now I, on the other hand, have been known to be charming, witty, and pretty good in the kitchen. So—"

She liked his smile.

"So you wouldn't mind fixing us some sandwiches," Peter said loudly.

"For her and I, yes, that would be delightful. Where do you intend to eat, Peter?" He chuckled.

Melissa blinked. Peter saw this and grabbed her by the hand. "Come on, let's go in the kitchen and fix the old man something. He can't cook worth a crap." Peter walked ahead of them. "When is Granpapa coming next?"

"You missed him. He's in Brussels right now and then he's going up north to Finland for something. Not sure what he's got cooking now."

The sandwiches were already made. Melissa guessed that all the idle chatter about fixing food was a running joke.

"Melissa is a computer consultant and has never been on the exchange floor."

His father stopped eating and his eyes lit up. "Really.

Well, we can do better than the exchange floor. I tell you what, ole Peter, you leave this young lady with me for a few days and I'll show her how the market really works, and you can go off and do, well, do whatever it is you do."

Peter stood between them. "Now, Father, she's my guest and I intend to show her around."

Melissa suddenly felt uncomfortable, as if this had happened before and was a family routine. "We could all go together, right?"

She played the part well—a perky young lady student, who really didn't care to understand how the stock exchange worked and only wanted to slam the gavel at the close of trading. The real dignitary of the day, an aging icon of finance, gladly handed over the gavel and she kissed him on the cheek. She giggled on cue. It was just three in the afternoon and the icon whispered he wanted to take her for a drink. As she walked across the small stage back to Peter, too many hands brushed various parts of her body. She giggled again, savoring the thought of these lecherous pigs wallowing in poverty when she was finished.

During the brief tour, she was able to walk through the trading floor after the final Friday afternoon bell. Melissa was disappointed to find the trading floor basically empty. She had envisioned a raucous and messy scene where traders were frantically trying to be heard making their final calls of the week. Instead, two groups of tourists in shorts and ugly shirts padded across the famous trading floor, gawking at computer monitors and television sets hanging from kiosks around the room. "It's all basically electronic?" She smiled.

"A couple of years ago they switched over to these monitors. Traders can enter orders electronically and don't have to be on the floor. It's a faster and more efficient system." This came from one of the old geezers who had been trying to touch her.

"And that system is well protected?"

"The Fort Knox of computer systems. No one can get in, guaranteed." When he smiled, the old man actually looked like a nice guy.

"I actually came to see Brett Douglass. He's expecting me."

The men became silent. It was like that when old men thought they were fawning over just another pretty young lady and discovered she was actually there to conduct business.

"Mr. Douglass, it seems, had a problem recently with your, uhm, Fort Knox security, and I was recommended to help him, if I can. Can you show me where his office is?"

сосо

Peter's father waved off the other men and lead her and Peter through the hallways to the administrative offices. Brett Douglass occupied a modest office with a grim view of the adjacent building. He was tall and probably had been a lean, fit marine at one time. But now was as wide at the hips as he was at the shoulders. His hand was rock hard as they shook, and she guessed he was solid muscle underneath the tailored suit. She noticed the photograph of Lieutenant Barnes on the wall—Barnes and Douglass in fatigues standing next to several destroyed military vehicles.

Melissa approached the photograph. "Operation Desert Storm?"

"Yep, right after the one-hundred-hour war, and just before we were told to turn around. We could have moved on Baghdad in five days and this second war we got ourselves into would never have been necessary." His voice was strong but strained from the many years of barking orders.

"And, now, here you are."

"Yes. I'm not sure what you know of this—"

"Look, this kind of crap bores the hell out of me. Peter, you and I need to talk, so let's leave these two alone. Brett, you know how to find me?"

"Yes, sir, I do."

"Fine you fix the geek stuff."

Brett closed the door behind them and sat back at his desk. "You run with an interesting set of people. You know who they are, right?"

"I'm learning."

Brett grunted and smiled. "You will never know even a fraction of the truth about them. Trust me."

The standard complaint of any manager of information systems was always, "They don't care enough to spend the right amount of money." The accountants responded with a risk matrix, showing the acceptable level of loss, and, given the predictions of the IT managers for loss, decisions were made to spend to the risk matrix. If the actual loss was greater than the IT manager had predicted, and was outside the acceptable level of loss, the IT manager was fired for incompetence. Somehow the accountants always survived.

Brett laughed as he recalled the budgeting process for the new IT systems. "They asked me what I needed and I gave them a comprehensive plan, scalable for anticipated growth for ten years, SOX-compliant security, and the capacity to handle three times the trading traffic given to me in the specs." He looked into the optical security scanner and waited for the green light. The door swung open for them. 'What I got was a set of tinker toys."

Melissa noted the hardware was perimeter centric, a

common mistake. It was always assumed there was a pimply face teenager in a basement in Minneapolis or a disgruntled rocket scientist in a failing former Soviet Bloc state, trying to steal data for survival money. No matter how many times she warned them, they always focused on the perimeter to keep these horrible people out of the computer systems, when it was common knowledge that more than ninety percent of all system cracking was perpetrated by someone on the inside, like Melissa.

"You trust everyone on the inside, right?"

Brett smiled and turned away. "We have to. You see what I have. The best I can do on the inside is to audit directory access. I don't have the manpower to watch the way I want to. Someone got the idea that our only risks were from the outside, especially after 9/11. They hired a big gun. He brought in a truck load of hardware for monitoring external intrusions and cut my budget for internal monitoring and performance. I like it when the guys on the floor or at the trading houses meet me and I tell them what I do. Their experience of my system is latency in the trade execution, and sometimes they even get bumped out completely in the middle of a hot trade. Oh, the foul language."

Melissa politely stood in the middle of the room, touching nothing. "It's pretty hot in here."

Brett laughed again. "Last week the chiller shut down in the AC room and, even with the server room door propped open, it was one-oh-five in here all day."

The technician sitting at the desk in front of the server looked up and shook his head.

"Nate here was in his underwear and still sweating." Brett motioned for Melissa to follow. "We do a great job of stopping external threats, but it is probably pretty obvious we are vulnerable on the inside. I was able to get the three different security doors. The first one we went through is a passkey given out to about fifteen people and they can get to the window to talk to Nate or another technician. The second door is a ten-digit code that the IT guys and then five of upper management have. The door with the optical is me, Nate, and Johnny only. No one else gets in there. That's the best I can do."

"The money traded to fuel the economy of the free world is behind three locked doors?"

"Yeah, if only I could get into Fort Knox that easily." Brett shut the door tight and tried it. It was locked solid. "I'd make some bling, bling out of a few of those gold bars." He held the door to his office open. "You want a drink?"

"Why not? It's Friday and the market is closed for the weekend. Scotch."

"You got it." Brett poured out two glasses and thumped them on the desk. He sat back down and looked out the window at a hot, muggy New York afternoon. "They'll all go up to the Hamptons, these captains of industry, and I'll be sitting here tomorrow and Sunday watching over their little treasure chest because they cut my staff budget." He raised his glass.

The two talked about some recent developments in security and the new hardware just out on the market. Melissa could see this was just banter and not what Brett really wanted to talk about.

She paused and set her glass down on the desk. "When we spoke, you said there was something urgent."

Brett turned back to face her. "First, let's check your pedigree. After I talked with Barnes, I called around. One of Nate's buddies went to MIT about the same time you did. One day you up and vanished, the rumor was something about hacking into the grade server." Brett set his glass down. "Now, that's not a deal breaker. I once hired a guy I caught hacking into my DOD servers and he turned out to be the best goddam network admin I ever had." He stared at her for a response.

"Unofficial penetration test of the system. The jackass who was managing the server hates women and dared me to do it, so I did. I even downloaded some porn into his profile and ran a scan that produced results directly to the CIO of MIT. Did they tell you about that one?"

Brett smiled. "Yes. And here we sit talking on a late Friday afternoon about a problem I have with securing the largest stock exchange in the world." He raised his glass. "I like honesty."

∽∾

Peter was waiting in the foyer of the administrative wing. Melissa walked up behind his chair but he didn't hear her until she was next to him.

"Can't you come in there?"

Peter cocked his head. "I wouldn't want to." He walked ahead of her, angry. "I don't go to places like that. It is taken care of for me. Not even my father goes in there. Those people in there, they are like sub-human or something."

"They are the security—"

"If my family depended on them to protect our money, we would be in a sorry state." He laughed and continued to walk ahead of her. "I mean look at the guy you were talking to. He's nothing more than a drone in the new army. They pay him just enough to buy a suit and rent a studio somewhere and his only job is to fix their computers."

∽∾

The walk back to the apartment was quiet. Melissa

now knew her place. She mentally repeated the words Brett had spoken when they first met. *'You will never know even a fraction of the truth about them. Trust me.'*

Peter silently let her in and handed her a set of keys. "I need to go with Father for a few days. You'll be fine here. The front door knows to let you in. If you need anything, just ask the maid."

"What's her name?"

"Who?"

"The maid. What's the maid's name?"

Peter looked at her and laughed. "I don't know. Ask her."

❧❧❧

The cool dry air of the Schultz summer compound was a welcome relief from the sticky heat of New York City. Peter's suite overlooked the larger of the two lakes. The children were already out, sailing mostly, and some were riding paddle boats at the far end. A few adults walked slowly around the edge, eyeing their children, yelling encouragement to the ones taking sailing lessons. Peter blinked twice and rubbed his eyes. Yes, he told himself, they were all naked.

Peter pulled on his jeans and a shirt and wandered to the dining hall for coffee. Everyone stared. He was dressed and they were not. His own father, who had flown in on a separate jet, was reading the paper on the patio, drinking coffee, naked.

"You've read this?" His father folded the paper. It was a German paper and Peter read it a bit slowly, not having used the language in a while. It was about the Schultz family and the loss of a granddaughter. The paper reported the cause of death was natural. The young woman had suffered from various heart ailments over the years and succumbed after a valiant struggle. By order of the family patriarch, she was cremated in Los Angeles and her ashes would be interred in the family mausoleum. None of it was true.

That was why they were in Germany. Armand Schultz was a second or third cousin to his grandfather. Peter quietly reflected on the fact he had killed one of his own relatives. He smiled.

His father grabbed the newspaper away from him. "Why are you dressed?"

෴

The funeral was a quiet Catholic Mass, celebrated in the family chapel. This time everyone was dressed. It was larger than Peter had remembered and he guessed there were at least seventy or eighty people comfortably seated. The suit they had placed in Peter's closet fit nicely. He sat next to the other male cousins as a pallbearer. They ranged in age from sixteen at the youngest to Peter the eldest. He was the only one of the six with dark ha. The others were flaxen blond with dark, tanned faces. The sweet odor of incense nauseated Peter a bit, but he shook it off.

The priest had arrived from Mulege the day before and suffered still a bit from jet lag. He had caught a cold, even in first class, and his voice was rough and loud. The Mass was in German and he spoke of the young lady, never mentioning her name, a custom in the family. He quieted his voice, acknowledging—not by name, but by status—the distinguished guests, and asked if anyone had words to say about the young lady. Armand looked around the church, nodding, and no one spoke.

Peter understood most of it. It was the usual fare of the will of God, heaven bound, and the rest. So much for the lie about cremation and the family mausoleum.

The six young men carried the casket out of the stone chapel. It was only then that Peter noticed members of other families, one in particular who would be a king one day. They carried the casket two hundred feet along the stone walkway to the entrance of the family cemetery, led by the priest and two acolytes dressed in red robes and white shirts. They placed the casket on the straps that would lower it into the ground, and the priest gave a solemn blessing. Two of the gardeners lowered the casket and the young lady's parents each threw a handful of dirt into the hole.

Everyone slowly walked out of the cemetery and back toward the main lodge to eat. They would never know Peter had carried his own victim to her grave. His objective of making a point was lost in the deep silence only money could afford. If Armand Schultz said it was a suicide, it would be reported as a suicide and no one would ask questions. Peter ate the fine food and drank the wine, chatting with everyone present, remembering past days of summer fun frolicking near the lake or winters on skis in the Alps. No one seemed sad for her, not even her parents. It was like when he was thirteen and there was a rumor one of the cousins in his own family had shot a young lady he was having sex with. No one asked questions. What good would it do to admit he had killed her if no one wanted to believe it was true? They would ignore him.

And what would become of him if he exposed these families, telling everyone how they really lived, what their real intentions were. He guessed they would never find his body and no one would ask any questions. He would be silent.

☙☙☙

As dusk settled into darkness, Peter walked calmly out of his suite and toward the lake. There were dim lights in the main hall. Some noises he remembered from his childhood drifted across the lawns. It was the part he hated the most. While the children slept, the adults would act out rituals handed down to them for ten or eleven generations. The funeral Mass was Catholic, but this was not anything like anyone on the outside would believe. The first time, he was forced to go. He was convinced a naked boy had been killed on the table. His father laughed and said it was just play acting, an illusion. The boy was fine. Peter never really knew.

Circumstances in his father's business life kept them away from these rituals until Peter was sixteen and he refused to go. His father had asked him tonight if he wanted to go and he said no. Nothing more was said. He wondered how much longer his father would tolerate him—perhaps until his grandfather died.

The warm, humid air embraced him. He wondered if people without money exercised these rituals. Probably. For most, this sort of thing would be a fad, a pop-culture experiment, rather than a cornerstone of their lives like it had been for these people.

He flipped over one of the paddleboats and slid it toward the edge of the lake. The moon was half full, but still bright enough to navigate out into the deep. As he steadied the boat, someone walked up from behind. It was one of the Schultz grandchildren, perhaps a cousin of the victim.

"You are going to paddle this alone?"

"Not if you want to join me."

"Yes, of course."

They climbed in the boat and quickly coordinated the paddling—slow, steady strides in rhythmic motion.

"To the island?"

Peter nodded.

The boat drifted slowly and bumped the edge of the dock on the manmade island. They tied the boat and sat on the dock, looking back at the lodge.

"Did you know her?' Peter asked quietly.

"A little. We met a few times, mostly while skiing. She is much older than me and, when I was twelve, she moved to the United States and I did not see her much. I had taught her how to ski." His accent was more noticeable now. "How do you know her?"

"We grew up at the same time. I spent many summers here. I think I remember you, but you were so young and I have not been here for so long. My grandfather and Armand Schultz are related somehow."

"All the people with money are related."

"And how are you related?"

"My father is Johann Schulz, son of Armand. I am Klaus Dieter Schultz." He extended his hand.

"Peter."

"Yes, I know who you are, and who your father is, and who your grandfather is. I even know about your great-grandfather and your great-great-grandfather, who were both here in Germany. I know your family owns many banks and hotels, much land, and even oil and many other things. I have been learning all about this since I turned eighteen and now have some of my money." Klaus Dieter paused. "How did you feel when you got your money?"

Peter smiled. "That was ten years ago. I felt very good then."

"Yes, I have had mine for only one year now. At first, I felt like Superman, but I realized that all the friends I make all my life, they are all like me. They all have money and, while we were such good friends, once we have our money, we no longer see each other. They are so busy buying cars, skiing, traveling on jets, and I am not so sure I want to do that."

"But you have to admit, growing up like this, it was better than some of the alternatives."

"I guess you are right. I have a lot of fun here, and in our other homes in the Alps. We ski so much in the winter. I often wonder what other children do."

"They do nothing. They watch television or play video games because they cannot afford to do this." Peter was quiet for a few minutes. "Why don't you go into the rituals?"

Klaus Dieter sighed and rolled his eyes. "You know what they do, yes?"

"Yes."

Klaus Dieter shook his head. "And you don't go."

"I did, until I saw what I thought was a murder of a boy about twelve years old." Peter lay back on the grass and looked up at the moon. "Has your family talked about politics much, and what they do?"

"My father and his brothers talk to my grandfather and his brothers often, but they do not include me."

For an hour, Peter told Klaus what he knew about both families and a few of the other families Klaus knew. Klaus looked at him, suspiciously silent, not reacting. They paddled quietly back to the shore in front of the lodge.

They returned the boat and walked slowly to the lodge. It was silent now, just a few room lights glowing. "You have said some very interesting things that are hard to believe, but they explain many things. When do you leave?"

"Tomorrow after the midday meal."

"I see." Klaus slowed his pace. "You live in New York."

"Not much. I need to be there now for a month. I

typically live in my motorhome in Nevada and California."

"Ah, yes. Las Vegas. I want to see that town."

"Come and visit me. Use this email address to tell
me when you are coming."

"I will come. My schooling does not start for another
month. I want to ask you more."

CHAPTER 19

Mark, Martha, and Derrick left before eight. Grady Junior left with his mother to help set up the conference room she was going to use for the board meeting. Grady poured more coffee and sat down at his desk. Vacations were overrated anyway, he thought. *Enjoy life as you live and vacations aren't really necessary.* Jeffrey had emailed him another sample of code he had found on the server. The style of the comments was the same and the code was written to capture internal passwords instead of customer account passwords.

He guessed the writer of both samples was educated in a large, well-known university. The style was what he recognized coming out of classically mathematics-based computer science programs—the comments were written in complete sentences. New, fast-paced career programming schools taught process logic, rather than math-based programming, and rarely stressed the need for comments to guide other programmers and software testers through the code. Trade school programmers were allowed to write cryptic comments or no comments at all and were graded on whether the program worked or not. This was usually because the instructor didn't know how to program and couldn't read the code.

He knew this from bad personal experience. His first programming class was a four-hour lesson in flow charting a logical sequence of events. One unlucky student was called on to diagram the logic of making a peanut butter sandwich. Grady figured that no matter where the poor guy started, it was the instructor's job to show him he had left out one or several steps and another victim was called on to fix the problem, and so on until the entire four-hour class had been wasted on bad process logic. He walked out of the class and the school and never returned. He arrived at Virginia Tech a week later and learned math-based programming.

He emailed the samples of code to a retired professor, Dr. Kahlil Rashid, he had studied under. Within the hour, the professor responded. He agreed it was from a traditional math-based computer science program and definitely a very intelligent student who had developed his own techniques for passing values in a more efficient method than was normally taught. Grady responded with appreciation and informed Dr. Rashid the code had been used to perpetrate theft of bank accounts. He attached the complete program. Dr. Rashid said he would pass it around to some of his peers to see if they recognized the work. Grady guessed this would take some time, so he grabbed his fly-fishing gear and drove to one of the more remote spots on the river.

After catching his limit, he went back to the cabin to clean the fish. He sat back at the computer to send the monitoring program he had promised to Colonel Burgess. He wrote a short note, reminding Mark that he might not like what he saw and to prepare himself for the worst. An email arrived from Dr. Rashid.

You should contact Dr. David Rohr, a professor of engineering at MIT. He expressed interest in the code and indicated it was very similar to that of a student who had been expelled.

Grady called the number Dr. Rashid had given him and Dr. Rohr answered.

"Dr. Rohr, it is very kind of you to invite my call."

"No problem, Mr. Marcs. Dr. Rashid indicated this was fairly urgent."

"Call me Grady. It is urgent to me, but not to the bank who was the target. Dr. Rashid said the program was similar to something you had seen previously."

"Yes, some years ago we expelled a student, a young woman, after she wrote a program very similar to this that searched for the passwords used by professors in the grading system. This young woman succeeded in altering the grades of several students, some for the better and some for the worse, depending on whom she liked." He paused to take a draw from a cigarette, then coughed. "I want to get your permission to show the program you sent to one or two of my colleagues here who were involved in the case."

"Please do. Let me give you a number where you can call me any time."

⍹⍹⍹

He had intended to get the groceries Sandy had asked him to buy, but the call came from Dr. Rohr just as he was walking out the door. "Dr. Chung is convinced it is the same woman. He taught her some of the efficiencies she used in her programming. We compared the sample you sent with the program she was caught using here and they both are very similar to the classroom samples Dr. Chung has on file. Her name is Melissa Eggers. If this is an official police investigation, we can open her student files with proper warrants, but other than confirming who wrote your code, without a warrant, we cannot help you beyond this. I am very sorry. We can clearly see that her intent in the code samples you sent is nefarious, but we live in such a litigious society our administrators would refuse to allow us to participate without the proper police documentation."

"Dr. Rohr, you have been most helpful. I don't think I will need anything from you at this time, but would you and Dr. Chung be willing to answer questions and perhaps even testify if it came to that."

"Of course." He drew on his cigarette and coughed.

After ending that call, Grady dialed Jeffrey's number. "What was the name of that contractor you told me about?"

"It's a company name, not a person. Because I am completing this audit, I have been trying to find out who owns it. The address we have on file is in Carlsbad, California, and the checks we wrote to them were cashed in a bank in downtown San Diego. Cashed, not deposited. The signature is a man's—Arthur Seward."

"That's a good start. By the way, why are you investigating this? You're an IT guy."

"Long story. Mostly to keep Sam out of it."

"Sam? What's going on up there?"

"Uhm, not sure if I can talk much about it. Call Charles. He directed me to do this. Talk to him."

"Yeah, fine. Do you remember the contractor who came on site?"

"Nope. Never met him."

"It could be a her."

"No, it was a guy. Gene kept talking about a guy. He would come in after midnight and leave before the morning. He definitely said it was a guy."

Grady needed access to Sam and dialed Charles number. He answered and asked if he could return the call in ten minutes. Grady waited, anxious to get to the store before Sandy returned. She would go on her own if he didn't do it and he would hear about it all night.

Charles called and apologized. "We are facing some internal problems here, Grady. Jeffrey said you called. I had asked him to investigate some expense reports he found hidden on the finance drive, and I did not want word out, especially in accounting. You never know who might be involved in something like this."

"Well, I have some information and wanted to work with Sam—"

"That's not a good idea right now. He sent some emails to Mary Reichert now that she's gone, and the information he sent is sensitive. You will need to work directly with me or with Jeffrey. I'm sorry, but this is just the way it needs to be for now."

CHAPTER 20

Melissa could see it was Brett's number just as Peter closed the door. Behind him was a young man, looking like he was in his late teens. Melissa waved and answered the phone.

"They tried again last night. They left a file on the honey pot server and it has an executable attached to it."

Melissa smiled. "Don't open anything. I'll be right there." She slapped the cell phone shut. "Much to tell you, but right now I have to run down to Brett's office. We're close."

Peter nodded silently, not smiling. "This is Klaus Dieter. He has a common interest with us. He will be staying with us for a while."

❧❧❧

Melissa loaded the program from the honey pot to a flash drive and opened it on an expendable laptop Brett kept for just such purposes. They had not locked the code and she was able to quickly ascertain what the objective functionality was—delete all data and program files. In short, eradicate the disk with a Department of Defense level scrub. With the backup system in place, the worst the NYSE would suffer would be a few hours of downtime and confusion, but the real damage would come after, when investors lost confidence in the electronic trading system. She smiled at their attempt.

Brett took the news with a curt smile. "The worst is the loss of confidence in the system. Any time these sheep, I mean investors, see a little wiggle in the stock market, they run like hell to the bond market and then to real estate. And when that tanks, they run back to the stock market." He glanced at the code she had printed out. "I don't know what I'm looking at here. Would you highlight the parts where you think this program would have done this? I mean, it's moot now, right? We got it in time?"

"Probably, but I would like to check the registry to make sure they were not able to leave anything behind. I need you to log in to domain controller as administrator."

"I'll just give you the password—"

"No, don't ever do that with anyone. I would also like you to stand behind me and observe what I am doing and then when I am done, log off."

Brett shrugged, switched his monitor over to the primary domain controller, and logged in. Melissa quickly accessed several file structures and scanned over them. She dialed into an FTP site, found the code for the "Bankers Delight," and moved it on to the domain controller. Brett was watching every move but she knew he had no clue what she was doing. "You're fine. They never made it beyond your firewall. Do you want me to help you prosecute?"

"Prosecute? No. Like you said, they didn't do anything."

"Well, technically, accessing someone's computer without their permission is illegal. We could easily prosecute."

Brett waved his hand and explained that his policy was not to worry senior management if there was no imminent danger. Any leakage of information about risk to the computer systems would send investors running. Any time there was an actual breach, the police always handled it very quietly, for good reason. If you wanted to see real pandemonium, people jumping from buildings, just leak out that the electronic systems managing trillions of investor dollars had been breached and accounts compromised. He shook his head, laughing.

Melissa laughed along with him. She had modified the program to execute on August fifth. At first, the program would document the entire NYSE computer system and log this documentation on a computer belonging to a very unsuspecting Muslim charitable organization. At will, Melissa could access these logs and determine how money was transferring from private funds, through brokerages to the companies who sold the stock. She would see how and when backups of these records were made and on to what media they were being stored. This would allow her to write a program later that would make it appear the backup process had been completed but in actuality the data was just deleted instead. She would have the option then of accessing accounts and diverting funds to other accounts, or she could simply convert electronic funds into nothing.

She also now had direct access to the domain controller when she needed it. It would be better if she could accomplish her goals without ever actively accessing her own program, but a failed mission might require brute force execution of a doomsday program that would destroy all financial records associated with the largest stock market in the world. She loved bad security architecture and trusting, ignorant people.

Brett had his hand on the small of her back as he escorted her to the main lobby. "I would like you to come back when you have a chance and look things over again. When do you leave town?"

"Well, I'm curious about something. There must be a thousand or more qualified security consultants in New York City who could have easily helped you out—"

Brett waved his finger. "Two things. First, I trust Barnes and he trusts you. Second, those thousand or more so-called consultants are probably watching the stock market more closely than you and me and, if even one of them found a credible security risk, all of New York would know about it in ten minutes and that would be the end of the New York Stock Exchange. I would never hire someone that had not been vetted by someone I trust absolutely and I would never hire someone who lives and works in New York. Period." Brett opened the last door into the lobby. "I don't understand technology all that well, but I do understand people."

"Well, I've got to get back to San Diego in the next few days, but why don't I make a point of coming out here in say early August."

"You sure? August here is hell. If you want to, that's fine, but I take off on vacation the fifteenth, and you won't have access after that until after Labor Day."

"Fine, let's set it up for the sixth of August."

CHAPTER 21

Summer didn't arrive in Seattle on the Solstice. The last weekend of June before Independence Day had always hit and miss, and this one was definitely a miss. The rain started as Grady drove over Snoqualmie Pass and continued all the way into the metropolitan Seattle area. This was a depressing contrast to the four weeks of sunshine and mildly hot weather in Wyoming. Grady had to remind himself of the promise he made to host the barbeque in Seattle on the fourth. Otherwise he would have extended the vacation.

Grady Junior knew better than to try and get out of any of the unpacking. The gear had to be properly stored, laundry done, and everything put away neatly and properly before he could even think of going anywhere.

Grady was silent for the duration. He had insisted on looking for a larger cabin while they were in Jackson Hole, but the conference took up all of Sandy's time. The best they were able to do was to meet for coffee with their agent and get her started looking. His comments about the rain from the pass into town were fairly nonstop and elicited only silence from Sandy. He knew he was aggravating the one issue that always prevented them from moving—her mother. Grady had what he thought was the only logical solution—buy a house big enough for her to move in. Sandy always wondered why he didn't see the obvious, that being moved to Wyoming would deny her siblings frequent access to visit her. His response was always the same. They didn't give a crap now, why would they care if she moved away? This was where the conversation ended. Sandy would glare at him and there would be silence.

The house was quiet after the chores were finished and Grady settled into his office. He opened an email from Mark Burgess.

Grady, got that software installed and you were right. This could be bad. One report showed me he uses chats a lot, and I started to record the chats like your instructions said and I need to talk so I can figure out what is going on. Mark

Grady dialed his number and Mark answered immediately. "Grady, thanks. I am stressing over this thing." He sounded angry and hurt.

"I warned you—"

"I know. Well, the first thing is he's chatting with another guy about sex. Okay, if he's gay, I have no problem with that. But, he's fourteen and the guy in the chats says he's sixteen, but he uses words and sentence structures like he's older, more like an adult. They are planning to meet here in town soon and I am just totally afraid of what this might be."

"Mark, you need to have that conversation now. Do not back down from this. Tell them everything and once you have done that, I need some information from you and I will find out who this guy is." Grady leaned into the phone. "Tell Derrick what I asked you to do and that this might be a trap. I can find out who he is in seconds. No reason to keep any of this secret now. If I find out this guy is an adult, we go to the police immediately."

Grady Junior was in his room and Grady asked him to join him in the kitchen where Sandy was cooking. "Mark is concerned about Derrick using chat to talk about having sex with another guy we suspect is an adult. If you know anything about this, tell me now."

"Yeah, Derrick told me he thinks he's gay. He found someone just like a year or two older and he's going to meet up in Dallas."

"Didn't your radar go off? Does the guy live in Dallas or is he flying in from somewhere?"

"I think he said the guy lives in Minneapolis or something like that."

"A teenager has the money to fly like that? I doubt that very strongly. What did you tell Derrick to do?"

"I didn't know what to tell him. He's afraid of telling his parents about being gay, so I guess he didn't want to say anything."

Grady nodded his head. "Mark Burgess won't care if his son is gay, period. He saw some really great rangers do extraordinary things and we found out later they were gay, and it didn't matter. The deal is this. Derrick cannot meet this guy. This smells bad, you agree?"

Grady Junior nodded. "Yeah, I wish I had thought about that."

"It's not too late. You email him and tell him that you and I and your mother have talked and you tell him what I think, will you? Tell him his dad is there to help him, not hurt him."

෴

The rain let up later in the evening, so Grady and Sandy went for a walk. The agent had emailed them two potential properties, and both looked good. One already had a mother-in-law apartment and the other could be easily converted. They had both been on the market for over six months so there was no hurry. Plenty of similar properties would be on the market so the choices were excellent. The only issue that remained was moving Sandy's mother.

"She won't move up there, especially in the winter. She's lived in Seattle for eighty-two years, she will never leave."

"I will charm her like I charmed you."

"Yep, for sure, she will never leave."

The call from Mark Burgess came just as they walked up the steps to the front door. True to his character, Mark had the conversation with Derrick and everything was fine with one exception. They had made arrangements to meet in a week in Dallas at the airport. Grady directed Mark to look at two reports he had written into the program and asked for the information. Mark read off an IP address, default gateway, MAC address, and then the hop count. He asked Grady what these were.

"This is the guy. I now know who his service provider is and exactly where he is located. I even have a neighborhood. What I am going to do next you should be unaware of. Keep your arm's length from this for a couple of days."

It was a static IP address, one given out to the same customer and never changed. He was able to associate the IP address with a website and without having to crack the user's computer got the name and address of Derrick's chat partner. It was a personal website and the photos were of a short, fat man in his forties. There was no mention of a family, just two cats and a dog. Grady ran a port scan and found a chat session open in real time.

He called Mark. "I need the IP address for Derrick's

computer. You will find it in that last report you read to me. And stay on the line with me for a minute." Grady confirmed the man was in a dormant chat session with Derrick. "Tell Derrick to do nothing with his computer for now." Grady easily spoofed Derrick's chat session and he was now in control of the two-way conversation. He sent the man a message.

Probably not safe to meet in Dallas. I've got some cash and can meet you in Minneapolis, and maybe we can go to your place.

There was a short pause and then a rapid succession of responses. Each one led up to a specific time and date to meet at the airport. Grady, still spoofing Derrick's account, confirmed the meet—two days from then, seven in the evening. He called Mark back. "I'm going to Minneapolis. You tell Derrick to tell this guy nothing. I don't want him to suspect anything"

芝芝芝

Grady took the call from Jeffery while he waited at the gate for his flight. He would see an email with more information on the contractor Gene Surrey had hired. It wasn't much, but there were two credit card transactions for meals at a security conference Gene had attended and Gene had dutifully written the initials of the person he entertained and the reason for the meeting. The initials were M.E. and Gene had scribbled she was a consultant.

Grady thought about this on the flight to Minneapolis. The trail was long and evidence very thin. Melissa Eggers had two dinners with Gene. She was probably trying to get the work, no matter for what reason. Everyone was adamant Gene had said a man had arrived to do the work and the money trail from there so far never touched Melissa. He could not physically place her in the bank until Gene Surrey decided to cooperate and no lawyer would let him, given the relationship he now had with them. He could easily implicate himself as a co-conspirator in the theft. Grady would have to find a connection between Melissa and the man who had cashed the check. It wasn't enough to connect student work similar to the programs he found on the bank computers. He would find her but, so far no, prosecutor would touch it. She was good, but not perfect.

Grady decided he would find her, document what he knew, and turn it back over to Charles. He would always remember her and the program she wrote, but her work might never cross his path again. He would send Charles a bill and spend the rest of the summer on some projects around the house with Grady Junior. It wasn't what Grady Junior was planning on for the rest of his summer vacation, but that was tough. If they were going to move, the Seattle house needed work before they could sell.

☙❧☙

Grady got a room at a small motel near the airport. All he needed was an Internet connection and a bed. He met Gregg Dorn, a Minneapolis police detective, in the restaurant adjacent to the lobby. He handed over everything he had and the detective was angry and frustrated. He knew the man was soliciting a minor, that was obvious, but the evidence was weak. Grady said he understood basic evidentiary rules, but this was for a friend, his former commanding officer.

"What branch?"

"Rangers. Spent most of our time together in Afghanistan before, and then after, 9/11."

Dorn picked up the pile of print outs and looked at it again. He read slowly and quietly. "I was a marine. Hated you bastards. Could have kicked your ass any day of the week half-drunk if we wanted. But that was all good fun. This is serious. Let me talk to my captain. You say this guy is meeting you at the Starbucks tomorrow evening?"

"And he's thinking I am fourteen."

Dorn shook his head. "Well, we need to put this guy on our radar. Let me call you in the morning." Dorn stood, shaking Grady's hand and started to walk away. He turned and looked back. "You probably would have made a decent marine."

⋘⋙

Dorn called at six in the morning, probably hoping to wake Grady, but Grady had already showered, eaten, and sent ten emails. "Meet me downstairs at seven."

When Grady got there, Dorn was waiting, pacing the lobby. "This is probably against every rule in the book, but we're going to take this guy in for questioning, even with the weak evidence, and see what we can shake out of him. He's got no priors of any kind and it's probably his first time going public like this. What you gave me isn't going to convict or anything, but we decided to just shake him up and let him know we're watching. You're lucky, the captain's father was a ranger. Korea. We will meet you here at six and go over some details of how we want it to go down."

⋘⋙

Grady was positioned at a table shared by the other food vendors in the airport, the Minneapolis police were at the newsstand and the taco bar. It was ten minutes before seven. The man bought what he had agreed to buy as his signal—a cookie and an iced coffee. He looked around. The detectives had left the newsstand and Grady began to sort and return papers to his briefcase. He looked at his watch, then quickly closed his laptop, and slipped it into the brief case. He slipped his ticket into his breast pocket and made it appear he was in a hurry to leave. The man settled in and appeared to decide everyone around him was just another passenger waiting to leave Minneapolis. Grady walked behind him and ordered a short latte—his own signal. The man began to watch him suspiciously and looked like he was going to leave. Grady sat down in front of him and slid a photograph of a knife across the small table to him.

"That knife belongs to Colonel Mark Burgess. He served his entire military career in the rangers and his preferred method of killing his enemy is with that knife. You, my friend, made the mistake of trying to arrange to meet his fourteen-year-old son in order to have sex with him."

Dorn approached from behind and placed his hands on the man's shoulders.

"That man behind you needs to talk to you, and I can assure you that, no matter the outcome of your conversation, if you ever contact Derrick Burgess again for anything, Mark Burgess will be the next person you meet. Do I make myself clear?" Grady stood to leave as the man was placed in handcuffs. He looked at Dorn and nodded. "Semper Fi. Have a great fourth."

"You too, Captain."

ფ~ფ~ფ

Grady explained to Mark the promise he had made to the man as they were arresting him. Mark laughed and thanked him. "What do I owe you?"

"For what?"

"The plane ticket to Minneapolis, the work."

"You owe me a copy of your book, and I want it for Christmas, so you'd better start writing." Grady turned his cell phone off and boarded his flight. Before they taxied out to take off, he was sound asleep.

CHAPTER 22

The priest was packed and waiting for his ride. Armand Schultz summoned him into a small waiting room near the main door. "Would you like something more to eat or drink before you leave?"

"No, sir. You have treated me like a king. I really appreciate being able to extend my visit." His cold was better and he sounded healthy again.

"You have enough funds? Are the finances okay?"

"Absolutely, sir. Again, I feel blessed to work with you."

"Fine. Fine. I have intentionally withheld information about my granddaughter's death from you, in the event anyone asked while you were staying here but, now that everyone is gone home, I can speak more freely. May I?"

The priest smiled and held his right hand out. "By all means, sir, please."

Armand smiled and hesitated. "Yes, of course. I think I am fairly certain how my granddaughter was killed. This was not a suicide, this was a murder and I feel strongly I know who has done this to our family. I know of a large financial transaction that went sour, it was a significant amount of money slated to influence some people and I stopped it all. Not out of conscience, but because they were bringing in the wrong people and I felt security was going to be breached. It was obvious I was the one who made this decision alone. I wanted it that way. The potential recipients of the money are skilled, as you are, and this was a message." He paused again. "If I needed a large action, say a coup or something, you know I have the resources for that. But it's not that this is a small, insignificant organization, either, but the use of brute force would not accomplish what I need here. You understand?"

"Absolutely, sir. You have various resources to respond to different needs."

"Yes, that is correct." The door opened slightly and Armand waved the driver away. "I am not certain what I want to accomplish yet, and I still need to complete a forensics exam and analyze the results. I just wanted to give you a little more information and thank you in advance if I decide to use you further in this matter."

"Sir, I am always available to you."

"Thank you. I have really appreciated your loyalty over the years." Armand opened the door and quietly shook the priest's hand. He hesitated. "Your brother called and was looking for you. I would like to keep good connections with him. I think I would find him very useful. Please give him my regards."

"I will see to that, sir. I'll call him from the car.

⁂

The drive to Hamburg and then the airport was smooth, silent, and air-conditioned. The priest thanked the driver and walked directly through the concourse to a door leading on to the tarmac and then to a waiting Golfstream GIV-SP. Attendants smiled at him and welcomed him. He walked up the stairs and determined immediately that he was the only passenger with two pilots and three attendants. It would be a nice flight back to Mexico.

After taking off, the priest approached the captain and asked if they could make an unscheduled stop to pick up a passenger in France. The captain said he would clear it with Armand Schultz and, if there was no objection from him, he had no problem with it.

"Will we have to clear Mexican customs somewhere? I've never flown into Mulege, always driven."

"I can land this in Mulege and there's no customs there, really. I checked when Mr. Schultz asked me to fly you there." The captain did not seem even slightly curious.

The priest sat back in his seat, a neat scotch now on the table next to him. The attendant smiled and offered to start preparing a meal.

"That would be delightful. That is very kind of you."

"My personal pleasure. I see the captain is motioning for you."

The priest moved to stand in the cockpit.

"Father, we have Mr. Schultz's approval to land in France. Will we need accommodations?

"Not at all. This will only take a few minutes."

"You want to land in Paris?"

"No. Caumont Airport in Avignon."

"I don't think I can land there without clearing it first. That's a military base."

"Yes, I think you can. You ask the flight controller if Colonel Nachman is waiting for us, and tell him his brother is taking him to Mexico. I think he will allow it. I've called ahead."

The captain nodded and began the process of gaining clearance.

As he ate the pate, the captain appeared in the cabin. "We've got clearance on one of the minor runways and Colonel Nachman will meet us there. We will have a military escort the last one hundred miles, of course. We should be there in about two hours, Father."

"Thank you. You are so kind."

Once on the Gulfstream, the priest and his brother, the colonel, spoke very little. It was friendly reminiscence, mostly, but little more. The priest made the obligatory offer of a place to stay in Mulege, but the colonel politely declined. He would need to be in northern Mexico, at Cuidad Juarez, within hours of landing in Mulege. A small plane would be waiting for him to complete the journey. Then he would be back in France and then Israel within twenty-four hours of that, before the Mexican government knew he was even in the country.

The priest nodded politely.

The landing in Mulege was smooth. The brothers shook hands and the colonel walked over to the small Cessna waiting for him. The priest thanked the captain and the attendants and they prepared to fly north to Tijuana for refueling before returning to Germany.

Martin was waiting in the Mercedes. "How is my grandfather?"

"He is fine. Fit, healthy, and always a gentleman. No doubt concerned over the untimely death of your cousin. You should go back to Germany and visit them."

"I would like to, but I don't think my grandfather would allow it yet."

"Maybe you're right. In time. In due time."

CHAPTER 23

S ins are heavy for those not adept at hiding them. A man with no conscience, who had hidden many sins, smiled through it all and slept well. But the beginner, who discovered the delights of forbidden fruit, was confronted with the problem of hiding the sin without knowing how. Some would discover a way, but most would find it necessary to confide, to share, and, hopefully, gain acceptance and forgiveness. These would never be good sinners or liars. They would always need to tell someone. Priests and pastors, while not well paid, could rely on a lifetime of employment, listening to these people recount their sins, pleading for forgiveness. Since they were human, they would sin again, especially the habitual sins, and they would scurry back to the confessional, promising to sin no more.

Peter knew he would kill again. He was well trained in the art of deception. He was able to feel without expressing that feeling. He could see the horror of his first murder, but he could also smile and sleep at night. He could see killing Klaus Dieter, feeling the horror of it, but it would be just another event he would willfully smile about, hiding any remorse and perhaps any sign of guilt. His grandfather had trained him well. Dr. Sutton would be proud. He could handle the trauma now. The boy in the fire was never really burned, never hurt. It was all an act. It was a well-planned metaphor. *Vicariously we deliver our fears of others into the fire and we can allow ourselves to be freed of this fear. It is nothing more than a ceremony designed to help us disassociate from the complexities of fear and anxiety and allow us to relax. Nothing more than realistic stagecraft. Bravo. Take a bow. Encore.*

Melissa flew back to San Diego and Peter bought another Lexus in New York to drive Klaus through the heartland. Peter enjoyed his youthful eagerness and intensity, leaning out the window as they passed through the poverty of West Virginia. Klaus was amazed at the conditions, bothered by them but, by the end of the day, ready for a decent meal and a nice bed. He understood the ratio concept. If Peter's father owned forty-three businesses employing one hundred thousand people, the raw materials and energy required to fuel these businesses required a tenfold number of people who mined the coal to power the plants. They worked on rotating shifts to refine the oil into gasoline to power the trucks and cars and to heat the homes, and the harder they fought to control the costs of these materials, the larger the profits. The goal, then, was to neutralize growth in wages and even seek out sources of labor that cost virtually nothing. Like prisoners who were so painfully bored with their existence being paid fifteen cents an hour to produce some of these raw materials or to manufacture small goods was a reward. Klaus suggested this was tantamount to slave labor, and Peter referred to it with the correct description—rehabilitation.

Klaus wiped his lips with the paper napkin. "And you like this system?"

Peter smiled. "Like? There's nothing to like or dislike about it. This is what we do." He laughed. "Your family, my family—this is what we do. We make money. And this is how you make money on a large scale."

∽∾∾

Since very few Americans would ever recognize his surname, Klaus was able to check into hotels without notice—a German tourist driving across the country.

"Good luck and stay away from the South in July. Gorgeous in the winter, but in July the heat is dangerously oppressive."

He could nod, smile, and thank them for the advice and no one knew who he really was. He didn't immediately understand the winks and smiles as Peter helped him unload their luggage. Later, he smiled about it himself. "You knew this already, what some people think of…uhm…us?"

Peter laughed. "This is America. We think funny."

"Well, of course, they never know, some of what they think might be true."

Peter liked the wry German smile, capable of appreciating the irony. He calculated the value of either killing Klaus as a more declarative statement or persuading him to help. Killing one of their women was tragic, but nothing that would stop that generation. Killing one of the men, one of the few men of any generation, was unthinkable.

Interrupting or even ending the male bloodline would be catastrophic. But Peter actually began to like Klaus and decided it was worth allowing him to live, for now.

In the gift shop of the Grand Ole Opry Hotel, Peter bought him an Elvis wig and some gaudy sunglasses for their trip to Graceland.

"Really, people dress up like Elvis when they go to Graceland."

Klaus tried them on, laughing hysterically in the mirror. "I need a white suit, with sequins."

"No, don't do that. They'd think Elvis was still alive."

Nashville was just as hot and sultry as everyone warned them it would be on the third of July. The pool was refreshing and Peter did not bother to warn Klaus about acceptable attire by the pool. He wore his small tight swimming briefs under his walking shorts and stripped down to them in front of fat, disgruntled men and gaping women.

Peter wore the same. The whisperings and grunts were audible and Peter ordered two margaritas. Later they ate steak in the bar watching a baseball game.

∞∞∞

Klaus thought there was some significance to visiting Graceland on the Fourth of July, Independence Day. One of the great icons of American culture and he was going to see the famous home on the very day America declared independence and established itself as the most power and wealthy nation in history.

Peter rolled his eyes.

The drive to Memphis was three hours and Klaus took careful note of the quaint names—Bible Hill, Oak Grove, Bucksnort, Sugar Tree, and his favorite, Blue Goose. "Between your country-western music in Nashville and the birth of rock and roll in Memphis, this state must be the most famous for music, even more so than the birthplace of Beethoven."

Peter looked over at Klaus. "Where was Beethoven born?"

Klaus laughed. "I don't really know." The lush green countryside rolled by. "This is truly the greatest country, and here I am helping you celebrate your Independence Day. I can't believe this."

Peter smiled and shook his head. "It won't be around for long, at least not the way you see it now. We are in a decline and before I am an old man it will be only a fraction of the country you see here."

"Oh, you know that is not true. Come now." Klaus leaned out the passenger side window.

"No, look, you're not really German any more, right? You are a citizen of the European Union." He could see the angry eyes as he glanced sideways at Klaus. He pushed a little harder. "I mean, now there is no difference between you and, say, someone from Paris."

"The French are pigs." Klaus's accent was thick, harsh, and quick now, not faint and smooth like he had practiced in language school. "I am not like the French. I am German." He rolled up the window and turned on the air conditioning. "The EU is nothing more than fat liberals sitting around thinking they run Europe when they do nothing. It is the German economy that drives the EU, our taxes pay their handsome salaries—"

"I know. I agree with you."

"Then why do you talk like this, like there is no difference between me and a Frenchman."

"I read an article about the guy, Branson, who owns Virgin Air? He has this thing he says. We are citizens of the world, as if there is no difference between a German and a Frenchman."

"My grandfather talks like this, like we are part Russian blood, part French, part English, like dogs, mutts you say. We are all the same and he says the same thing—we are citizens of the world."

"Exactly, but who are they really referring to? Who

are the people who can afford to be world citizens, have homes in nine different countries, be able to fly at will between these homes, and live as if there were no boundaries? Is it the people we saw in that Wal-Mart?"

Klaus smiled and shook his head. "No. It is you and me. I can fly anywhere I want."

"Right. And my family owns homes in ten different countries. We don't care about national borders. We own companies in twenty-five countries. My father can call up the President of France and schedule dinner with him. Let me ask you this. Who really benefits from the European Union? The average German citizen?"

"No. My family does, however."

"Yes, that's right, and so does mine." Peter laughed. "The more economies are the same, the more money we make."

e/ɔe/ɔ

As Peter predicted, there were several Elvis imitators waiting in line to tour Graceland, some more convincing than others. Klaus had decided not to be one of them. Two stood in sharp contrast to the fifty or so others waiting, who were mostly white Americans in shorts and tee shirts, large stomachs protruding out, laughing and talking loudly. Klaus was six feet, four inches tall, and Peter was the same. One was blond and the other had short, jet-black hair, and both looked desperately thin standing next to the others. They didn't fit, but they paid for the tickets and took the tour anyway. This is what Klaus had come to see. He was a little disappointed at the lack of opulence he had been warned was such a central part of the Elvis experience. "If you want real opulence, go look at some of those wasteful old churches in Bavaria. That is opulence."

৩৩৩

It took four days to drive across the prairies, through the Rockies, and then up through the Sierras at Yosemite National Park. There were only a handful of hotel rooms available in the park, all of them expensive suites, and they took one. The price did not seem to affect Klaus and he did not try to negotiate. The desk clerk raised her eyebrows when Peter stood next to him and she turned away scowling. Klaus was confused.

"Don't worry about her. You will find people like her everywhere. She thinks we are gay because you just paid a thousand dollars for a room and you are with another handsome guy. Just like back in Nashville at the pool, and then at the other hotels. When two handsome young men, who can afford nice things, travel together, everyone assumes they are gay."

"But why was she so disturbed by that?"

"Probably Christian. Or maybe Mormon."

Klaus looked even more confused.

The bus tour of the park took two hours and, after they ate lunch in the hotel, Peter promised Klaus he would drive him to the summer camp where they would meet up with his father. He warned that, on the map, it looked like a short distance from Yosemite to Sonoma, but it would take upward of five hours to get there. They were in California now.

৩৩৩

The Sonoma Valley reminded Klaus of parts of Germany near the French border. They drove several miles out of town and arrived something called the Bohemian Grove. The guard at the first gate took Peter's driver's license and made a phone call. He immediately returned the license and handed it back. "Thank you, sir, and have a nice time."

The room they shared was the same room Peter had slept in as a boy. He smiled at the thought of how disturbed he would have been as a ten-year-old boy to return to the room, but now, trauma was a natural state in life and he just lived through those moments. In fact, there really was no trauma when you put it all into perspective. If you were traumatized, then you were being controlled. The ones in control inflicted the trauma.

CHAPTER 24

Grady Junior was up and ready when told to be. Breakfast was fast and Grady sat in the passenger seat, waiting. Grady Junior checked for his permit, knowing his father would ask, and presented it as he fastened his seat belt.

Grady answered his cell phone. It was Lieutenant General Sean Donnelly, United States Army Tactical Operations Center.

"Marcs, I have a problem. Data com in the C2V systems is shitty. I need someone who can fix this goddam thing. I thought for a while it was them jamming us, but it's the software in this goddam system. I need you to take a look."

Grady Junior started the engine and Grady shook his head.

"I know the guys over at General Dynamics. They're pretty sharp and they wrote that code. What's wrong with them?"

The integration of C2V data communications systems in the Stryker Brigade had been well planned and well executed but was now a victim of internal politics.

Anytime a good system was implemented, the owners always wanted immediate improvements and upgrades, even before the developer had worked out the bugs on the original system. Grady was happy he did his code writing as a member of the forces and not as a civilian contractor. The security work was great, but civilian developers were notoriously at the mercy of the conflicting agendas of generals and presidents. On top of that, computers were never fast enough for the military brass.

"Someone over there got caught with some sensitive stuff on a laptop he left behind on vacation. The investigation might take a while and, rest assured, the brass wants to proceed with or without them. And if they are under investigation, it's without them."

Grady agreed to call the colonel in charge of the program and decided he would do anything to avoid getting between the army and General Dynamics. He waved at Grady Junior to continue. The bank problem was going nowhere and he was a day away from calling Charles Greely and dropping all of his materials at the front desk. If they didn't want to report a crime, Grady wasn't going to chase down some college dropout chick. Then he would need some cash flow to pay for the house repairs without dipping in to the investments. There might be a way to prove helpful to General Donnelly and stay out of General Dynamic's way.

His concentration shattered when an SUV blew a stop sign and Grady Junior slammed on the brakes.

"Good eye. That guy didn't slow at all." The cell phone rang again. It was Charles Greely. Grady motioned for Grady Junior to pull into a parking lot and wait. "Charles, how can I be of service?"

"I've had a conversation with the FBI about a few things and wondered if you might be available to help us both out here. They need some technical information and

I don't want to spread too much around the other employees right now."

Grady smiled. Legitimate billable hours and Greely had grown some balls.

"I'm busy today. Can you set something up for tomorrow?"

"I already have. I'd like to talk with you at nine and then they are coming over at ten."

"Can I prepare anything ahead of time?"

"We're looking into some things involving Reichert and Surrey. Think about how we can retrieve data they may have deleted or how to prove they deleted the data."

"Okay, having been in there, I know the system and how little Surrey did for tracking access to sensitive data bases. Is Jeffery out of the loop on this?"

"Today, yes, but maybe we can discuss his role tomorrow."

"See you at nine." Grady slapped the phone shut. "Let's get going. No more calls."

Grady left instructions for how he wanted the back deck torn up. He hired two of Grady Junior's friends and told them he would pay cash at the end of each day. They were busy removing the three-inch decking screws when he rolled out of the driveway at eight-fifteen.

Charles Greely was alone in the conference room. He slowly laid out some documentation with the admission he was not in a position to interpret it fully. Mostly, they were access control logs and the information in them was cryptic at best. "I can read any kind of spreadsheet with financial data." He smiled weakly. "But this is new to me. I need to find out how much both Reichert and Surrey knew about the thefts and this is what Sam Wilkerson gave me."

Grady read though the logbooks. "If you recall the day I met you, this is what Gene Surrey was reading from

and, even then, I didn't know how he had configured his
log management. I needed to know what he set his system to look for and I wouldn't feel bad, if I were you, because this is gibberish to me as well." Grady flipped
through the logbook for a few moments. "Where is Sam
on this thing? Is he in the loop?"

Greely shook his head slowly. "No. Sam is on leave.
I told him to get an attorney."

"Then you may need to dispose of me as well since it
was Sam who brought me in on this and I see a conflict
of interest proceeding."

"I don't. Sam is involved in something else. He had
nothing to do with this. His problems are of a personal
nature and have nothing to do with you or the bank."
Greely leaned back. "I considered all of this. This is why
you haven't heard much from me lately. Right now, I
need to find out what you know of the thefts and then
we'll tell the FBI what I want to tell them."

"I don't like the sound of that, Charles. If Sam told
you anything about this, I know he told you I operate
transparently or I don't operate. If you want the truth and
then you proceed to deceive the FBI, then I cannot be anywhere near this investigation going forward." Grady
stood to leave. "If you want what I know, I will write a
report, attach my bill for services, and we will be finished. What you do to my report is entirely up to you."

"This is the second time you've done this. Let me
explain something to you and then see if you want to
leave."

Mary Reichert had been under investigation by the
FBI for securities fraud. The investigation had begun
several months before any of the thefts, and Greely considered them a separate issue and wanted them investigated as such. He had been through many of these inves-
tigations when young agents with more gusto than brains

had tried to lump too many similar events together into one investigation and succeeded only in creating muddy water and never really prosecuting effectively. In his first meetings with the FBI, he had hoped for a more seasoned team, but considered what he had and decided he needed to be careful to keep the issues separate. The FBI matter involved manipulating the value of the stock and the matter of covering up electronic theft of funds and security incompetence and was an entirely separate and unrelated matter. "You came in here assuming I wanted to continue the cover up. No. I want to make sure we investigate both matters separately and thoroughly."

"Who are the local agents on this?"

"Special Agents Matt Grantham and Sherri Edwards." Greely smiled. "Edwards has an MBA and I think understands. Grantham knows shit about banking. Do you see the problem?"

Grady sat down and began to detail everything he knew about Melissa, the consulting contract, how the money was laundered through a San Diego company, and her code.

He again admitted he would need to spend several hours deciphering Gene Surrey's configurations of the logs, and most usefully with Jeffery, before he could give anything definitive to the FBI.

Charles sat silent for several minutes. "Okay, here's my idea and then you tell me if you can do this. I will have you in the room for a discussion about our internal investigation into the thefts. You can give as much or as little detail as you like, but I will end that part of our discussion with an explanation that our internal investigation is not complete and we are not sure whether we want to proceed with a criminal investigation, based on the advice of our attorneys. If they want to ask questions, they will have to do so with our attorneys present. I will then ask you to leave so you are not party to any of the securities fraud investigation."

✧✦✧

Special Agent Matt Grantham was not happy. As predicted, he wanted to ask questions to determine for himself if the issues were related. Special Agent Sherri Edwards advised him to let the matter drop as she did not see any relation between the matters. Grantham iced over and asked her not to speak until they were alone. Greely thanked Grady and excused him.

Jeffery was waiting in the lobby. "Charles just called me and asked me to meet you before you left. Something about the access control logs."

Grady left very detailed instructions about how he wanted the logs collated and labeled. He asked Jeffery to reinstate his account on the network and allow him to network in from home. He thanked Jeffery, left the bank, and then headed for the Seattle office of the Federal Bureau of Investigation.

✧✦✧

Jimmy Steele no longer bothered to use titles or rank designations. To everyone in the Seattle office of the Federal Bureau of Investigation and most other offices around the country he was just Jimmy Steele. Even the director, when presenting him with a service award, forgot his true title and simply referred to him as Jimmy. Grady presented himself at the front desk and asked for him. The guard called and then waved Grady through.

"Who is this Matt Grantham?"

Jimmy smiled and took his feet down from his desk. "The newest moron."

"What's he doing in bank fraud?"

Jimmy looked at him, shaking his head.

"Just walked out of a meeting over at Northwest Bank and Trust with him and another agent, uhm…"

"Edwards. Miss Sherri Edwards." Jimmy rolled his eyes. "They had nowhere to put him so they stuck him in the highest position he could never possibly succeed in. He was a narco, pretty good at it because most of the people he arrested were probably his friends. He did kiddie porn for a while, but was too violent on the suspects and lost a lot of cases that way, so they moved him up. But bank fraud. Wow. I'm further out of the loop than I thought." Jimmy leaned forward on his desk. "What do you want?"

Grady sat down without being offered. "I've got a case going with Northwest. Someone slithered in through an unsecure server and stole two million from personal accounts. It's all covered with insurance and Charles Greely, the CEO, wants to keep it quiet for a while, for obvious reasons. He wants to keep the securities fraud thing separate and I agree, but I don't agree with keeping the account thefts silent."

"What do you have?"

Grady laid out the case against Melissa Eggers, including the consulting work, the delayed trojan on the server, the nature of the code, and how he identified who had written it. He gave names and dates of the money trail. Jimmy wrote quickly and thoroughly.

"No motive? Notes, letters, threats?"

"None, yet. Maybe nothing more than theft."

"Why are you giving this to me?"

"I smelled Grantham's incompetence and I will not be involved in a cover up."

"Does this guy Greely know you're here?"

"Nope and I want to keep it that way."

"Good. I'll bet he's involved. If he's not, I don't like the way he does business. I'll work on this personally and let you know if we're interested. You know what I can share and can't."

Grady stood to leave. "No problem."

Jimmy leaned back in his chair. "Jack says you hired him to tear your deck apart with Grady Junior. It's about time you helped clean up the neighborhood."

"Moving on. Jackson Hole. It's time to get out of this racket. That is if I can get enough out of the house."

"Yeah, I agree. I could walk out of here with full pension now, but Susan has another two years to go." Jimmy looked out the window. "What's in your gut on this thing?"

"It's bigger than just one gal stealing a little money."

⌀⌀⌀

Jimmy liked to take a walk, instead of eating lunch. Downtown Seattle had steep hills and he would walk a grid up the streets, then down, across a flat area, then up again and down. He never walked the same pattern, but always walked a full hour every day. He liked walking in the rain, and even the snow when it came.

Jimmy was the same way about his church, his family, his bills, and everything he owned. Do it correctly. Do it on time. His son, Jack, was beginning to develop the same traits. Jimmy had never lectured him, just did the right thing every time, on time, and he knew his son would want to be like his dad.

He did not like drivers who cut pedestrians off in cross walks. He would bang on the trunk of the offending car. The driver would inevitably stop and he would flash his FBI badge and shake his finger at the driver, always to the delight of any other pedestrians around.

Back in his office, he would open the brown paper bag, his wife LaToria would pack every morning, and devour the sandwich, fruit, and two cookies he ate every day. Now in his late fifties, younger agents with master's degrees in a variety of sciences, and even psychology, nipped at his heals, ridiculing the old man with no significant post-secondary education who wore his shoes until there were holes in the bottom. What he knew were the inner circles of the FBI. He knew the history. He had worked under Old Man Hoover and the younger ones never knew this. If they did, like his peers, they would back off. But he never told them and he enjoyed their pathetic political games. He knew how to handle them, what to know about them. He hated the gossip about Hoover. They hated him because he knew how to handle anyone who crossed his path. He liked the fact that Hoover had handpicked him, and he became, at one point, one of the most powerful black special agents in the FBI and, ultimately, chose Seattle over DC for his family.

CHAPTER 25

Melissa dressed nicely for her trip to the base. Colonel Bartle had called and wanted to chat. This probably meant another case. She stepped out in the cool morning air. Mid-July in San Diego was usually perfectly balmy, the really hot weather coming later in September and October when the Santa Ana winds began. She noticed a nondescript car following for a while and stopped at her neighborhood coffee shop. The car passed by, two men looking ahead and not at her. She sat for a minute in her car, sipping the latte, looking around. She was satisfied and drove directly to the base.

By the time she was waved through the gate, she was ten minutes late, something Bartle hated. He was sitting with his elbows on his desk drinking coffee. "I guess when I retire and become a civilian, I will have to develop this habit of being late all the time." He emphasized "all the time."

"Sorry, sir, I didn't account for how busy it would be at the gate."

"I got a call about you. Someone was inquiring about your security clearance."

"Who?"

"I thought you could tell me. You've done everything you need to do keep your security clearance active, right?"

"I think so."

"Wrong answer."

"I'll make sure."

"You do that. Now I've this other thing going on." He pushed a file across the desk. "Ordinarily, I would just give it to NCIS and let them play with it, but I want to know something about this before I hand it over to them. It involves a friend and I want the truth, good or bad."

"Okay." Melissa sat down an opened the file. Major Paul Markum was being accused of harassing black marines in an Internet chat room. Transcripts of the chats showed someone was using a pseudonym of Major Screwup. This nickname was given to him by his CO, Colonel Jerry Bartle. The complaint came from two black marines who felt Major Markum was specifically targeting them. Colonel Bartle was not suspected of this activity, but the complaint against Markum stood.

"No one knows about this and you report directly and only to me on this. If NCIS gets wind and asks questions, refer them to me."

"Definitely, sir, this will be pretty straight forward. Any preliminary thoughts?"

Bartle shook his head, saying nothing. Melissa nodded and left.

ఴఴఴ

Melissa drove north to Carlsbad and stopped in front of a strip mall of small shops and two restaurants. She telephoned Arthur Seward. Bonnie Seward, his wife, answered. No, he wasn't in. He was out for lunch. Yes.

Bentley's. Melissa searched for their number in her phone and called. Yes, Mr. Seward was there. Yes, it would be possible to bring the phone to him. No, he didn't use cell phones. Who was calling, please?

"Melissa, my dear. How is my stunning daughter?"

"Daddy, someone was calling about the security clearance. I went to the base to look at more work and the base CO told me he got a call and doesn't like it. He didn't say who it was."

"Simmer down. They do this every year, just trying to see if I am still in business. Where are you?" He was seated at his favorite outdoor table at Bentley's, a tall man with a shock of white hair and handsome in his classic blue blazer and gray slacks.

"In Carlsbad, I called Bonnie and she said you were there."

"Come for lunch. Chin and Boyle are here and they would love to see you."

Arthur Seward, John Chin, and Devon Boyle had all met in Da Nang in 1972, their third tour in Vietnam. The United States was already on the run and it was apparent the war would be over soon. There was so much perfectly good military equipment abandoned in several locations, the three decided to simply steal it, sell it, and ship it anywhere they could find a customer. They used compromised personnel in the diplomatic corps in Saigon as couriers of photographs and written descriptions of the materials and soon had customers all over South East Asia, the Middle East, and Africa. Spreading around a few thousand dollars to corrupt dock masters gave them access to ships and loading equipment and, within six, months they thought they were rich. After investing in seaside real estate in northern San Diego County, they developed the properties slowly, wisely amassing real fortunes. Their reputation for knowing who had stolen armaments from the Vietnam era allowed them to contract to army intelligence under their partnership to repatriate the equipment to the United States. Their job was to find the rogue elements who had secured these armaments and bring them to justice. It was a turkey shoot since they were all former customers who bought the weaponry from them in Vietnam. Being the daughter of Arthur Steward and, therefore, an employee, allowed Melissa to gain and maintain her top-secret security clearance.

Today was John Chin's sixty-second birthday and they all lived within a mile of Bentleys. Melissa arrived and searched for the trio, finding them in the shade. After the kisses and ordering her favorite stuffed Portabella mushrooms, Melissa hugged her father and flirted with Chin and Boyle.

Arthur became serious for a moment. "The money from the consulting is raising some eyebrows. There's a lot of it."

"I charge a lot of money."

"The trail, though. Aren't you worried?"

"I fixed the trail. There is a guy by the name of Gene Surrey at Northwest in Seattle. All the money from the private accounts is traceable to him, then it vanishes in a series of off-shore accounts and ends up in your Bahaman account. Mr. Boyle takes it from there, right?"

Devon smiled. "We have invoices for recovering and shipping a boatload of rocket launchers and these are shown being as received by army intelligence in Frankfurt. There's about forty degrees of separation. The only traceable check from Northwest was the one for twenty grand. That's peanuts and I needed something traceable to look legit."

"Yes, you two have always been careful." Arthur turned to Melissa. "You were in New York. What do you have there?"

What she had was a messed-up guy with billions of dollars at his disposal who had the social connections that had gotten her behind the firewall of the New York Stock Exchange. To her father, this would look like a heist and he would want to know about the money trail. He might even balk at the prospect of attacking something so important. It would attract attention like they had never known and he and his partners would object. Like her father, she saw opportunity, but hers was on a very grand scale. She would be wealthy beyond imagination and her other objective of hurting the elitists who were running this country was easily in her grasp. She would send only a very small fraction of the funds to her father and his partners.

"It's a small, regional bank. I met their CIO at the same trade show and he wants me out there again in early August. I'm thinking they're worth one or two million. Normal split."

Devon Boyle was tapping on a Blackberry and nodded. "When do you think the funds will start to pass through the system?"

"Mid-August."

"Okay, I will get some invoices made up, and I'll just need to know, usual channels, how much you're putting into the system."

Her father patted her leg. "You should really find a way to transfer funds from the really wealthy instead of these small time accounts. I mean, I hate putting the working people out. We're just working people like them and I'd hate like hell if someone took a thousand dollars out of my account."

"Daddy, it's insured and they're covered."

"I know, but it's just the damn inconvenience."

"I'm working on it, Daddy."

"That's my girl." Arthur started to eat. "Now about

the security thing, we'll take care of that. I'll have lunch with Bartle's CO and tell him to quiet it down."

౿ఎ౿ఎ

The message from Brett Douglass was short and somewhat terse. Bartle had called him and told him of the security clearance review. Brett wanted a call back immediately. Melissa listened as Brett weakly blamed "upper management" for their concern, and wanted to schedule a conference call as soon as possible. She returned the call, telling Brett she had just met with her other partners and this was a routine audit of their business arrangements with the Department of Defense, and part of that audit was a review of security clearances. He liked what he heard and said he would get back to her about the conference call.

Brett hung up and walked into the server room. Nate was sitting on the stool in front of the authentication server in just his running shorts. He motioned Brett to take a look at the strange file he had found tucked inside a rarely used folder. It was encrypted and could not be opened, and they could not determine when it had been placed there.

"Show me the file this woman Melissa worked on." Nate walked over to the laptop they had used to open the file originally. It opened quickly and the date and time stamp of the last use of the file was exactly the time when Melissa had helped determine what it was. "This is the only thing she did here, right?"

Brett nodded. "Thanks, Nate. Please work on that encryption. I want to know what it is. If you can, just move it to this laptop and remember to never connect it to any NYSE domain."

Nate moved the file, but was unaware of the copy

that had been automatically generated. This file would appear somewhere else in the domain, and perhaps they would never see it. Moving the copy would automatically generate another roaming copy. They could remove the file as much as they wanted until it actually executed on August fifth.

Melissa thought this was a beautiful thing and was proud of her work when Brett asked her about it. She told him to keep it isolated until she got there on the sixth and wondered if they needed to have the conference call. Brett said he would get back to her. Melissa offered to help Nate decrypt the file. Brett thought that would be a good idea and gave her the server room number.

Nate was kind and co-operative, but it was evident he was not skilled enough to understand completely what she had done. She tested his encryption knowledge and determined she could easily send him a crack for the encryption that would also alter the content of the file. She promised a crack by the next morning and advised him to move the file immediately.

ひそひ

Colonel Bartle sent Major Markum on a day-long errand. Melissa arrived at nine, long after he had left, and spent an hour examining his workstation. She found several saved chats and evidence he had actually logged into the forum. She did not find anything on his computer that would indicate he had written the hateful messages. In fact, the messages she found were primarily of a religious nature and typically very positive comments about other members. She ran a quick password crack and had his password to the forum within fifteen seconds. His password was "GOD."

Colonel Bartle smiled. "It's not him, is it?"

"Nope. Someone who knows him well, however. I want to go to the administrators of the forum and ask if they can tell me what IP address those messages came from. I really don't think he did this."

With half an hour she had both the IP address and the Mac address of the computer the message had been sent from. Bartle ordered Lieutenant Barnes to scan the network for those addresses and he had them in a few minutes. They were associated with a workstation used by Markum's former secretary, a corporal who had received a poor review.

Bartle quickly gathered the paper evidence, placed it in the original file, and dialed the number for NCIS. "Is there anything else, Ms. Eggers?"

Melissa smiled and left his office.

CHAPTER 26

Peter wondered, if it was so easy to inflict death, then what was to be said of the quality of the life preceding that death? Was it worth anything? To the living, perhaps. A father who earned more money than the mother would be sorely missed. A young soldier killed in war left behind a sorrowful mother, a crying girlfriend, brothers and sisters who would always remember him at the height of this youthful strength. The heir to one of the largest fortunes in Germany would be missed, especially because he has no brother and the family name would cease to exist. The smooth, handsome face of this heir, this Aryan delight, this innocent young man who would grow up to adopt the same goals and aspirations of his family of the past two thousand years, was beautiful in the moon light. Peter wondered if, in the end, life was forced out or taken.

It was to be the last days of the trip and they would spend them in the motorhome, by the beach. Klaus would enjoy one last piece of Americana—surfing. For two days, he donned the skin-tight wetsuit, packed the surf board across the highway to the beach, and took his chances as best he could. He fit in. Tanned, blond, and tight he looked like every other American on the beach. They smiled at him and he returned the smile. They could see he was a beginner and showed him how to roll the edge, lean forward, then back, and how to take a fall into the deep, salty water. Peter watched it all, smiling.

A group of them were drinking in an Italian restaurant by the beach when Peter and Klaus went to dinner. Peter invited all of them to eat. Fifteen of them sat around the table and ordered what they liked and Klaus paid, in cash, and this they would talk about for years. Peter knew surfers were a cheap lot. They would have been perfectly happy stealing happy hour food left behind by the well-heeled patrons and drinking late into the night, but the prospect of a full menu dinner paid for by someone else was rare and relished.

Everyone was either very drunk or a little tipsy, except Peter. His mind was clear, cold, and focused. He helped Klaus up the awkward steps of the motorhome and sat him gently in an easy chair. Klaus mumbled happily, but was soon passed out. Peter poured himself a scotch and looked at this distant cousin, the perfect Arian. His face was smooth, handsome, and perfectly proportioned. His hair was waxen blond. Peter stripped him of his clothing, finding a hairless, tanned, and toned body with a small patch of pubic hair. Hitler would have loved him. Peter helped him into the bed, covered him, and went back to finish his drink. He set the glass in the sink and undressed for bed.

Klaus stirred. Peter sat back in the chair beside the bed. He held a short, jagged-edged pocketknife in his right hand.

Innocence was lost by choice, mostly. Boys grew up to become the evil they so despised in their youth. As young men they were so righteous. They saw all the wrongs and, as adults, they committed them. They swore they would never be like them, never trust them, and now they did every bad thing their elders did and more. When innocence was lost in one generation, the next would out-do it and lose not only innocence but the very notion of it.

Peter watched Klaus move his hands up and down his body, fully asleep, an involuntary nocturnal reaction.

It was rare for a grown man to reject evil. Boys be-lieved in Jesus, men in their money and the power it pro-vided. There was nothing else for either of them. If you didn't have one or the other, you were truly nothing. You wandered nameless, no more than a drone owing money and favors and time with your children. You gave Jesus to your children because you had nothing else. If you had money, you would give them that instead, early on, so they knew what they were in for. You gave them the ster-ile cold of an existence fearful of loss and death. Every-one wanted to take your money, but if you had Jesus they left you alone. You taught your children one thing. The Gideons handed out the Jesus book for free, but money was harder to come by and must be protected, at all costs. And, if it was not growing, it was shrinking and would, eventually, go away. It was tangible and real. That was the nature of money and that was the nature of existence for those who had it. Jesus, on the other hand, could not be seen or heard.

Peter smiled.

Klaus mumbled something. Peter listened. It was a love poem. A sweet child's love poem, in German.

He will inherit billions and he lies in bed, reciting children's poems. Who decides this thing about money? Peter twirled the point of the knife on his thumb and sucked the drops of blood. Partly, he wanted to do it to spare this beautiful boy from his destiny and, partly, he wanted to show it could be stopped. Kill the men and the name would die. Peter wondered how many families stopped existing after the wars. He laughed. If only the rich went to war, they would all die.

Klaus woke and looked up at him, startled at first, but then he smiled, bright white teeth reflecting in the dark. "Have you been sitting there all night?"

"No, I just woke an hour ago and wanted to watch you sleep."

"Did you like what you saw?"

"Very much. May I sleep with you?"

Klaus shrugged. "Of course."

Peter folded the knife and set it carefully on the table by the bed. He slid under the covers and was careful to lay flat and apart. Klaus was soon breathing that low, steady breath of sleep. Peter turned his head and watched this young Arian beauty peacefully breathe the air of the privileged and the powerful. Maybe it would be him or maybe his own son who would finally effected the domination of the masses. Peter wasn't going to take any chances. He unfolded the knife and, in the dark, felt the short serrated edge biting against his thumb. He moved silently toward the breathing Arian and held the edge against the throat. He moved with too much force and dug deep enough into the neck to strike the bone. There was gushing blood, gasping of breath, and thrashing of arms and legs as the Arian, in pain and the final throws of life, tried as anyone would try, instinctively, to preserve the life that was flooding out of them. It was over within seconds. The lungs gave a grinding gasp. The warm blood filled every crevasse in the bed sheets and covered Peter's arms and legs. He breathed in that smell, the smell of blood and shit and death. He folded the knife and got out of bed to shower. He hated Arians.

ɛ෴ɛ෴

Peter wrapped the body in blankets careless of the dripping blood. He thought of where he would dispose of it. No one would think of coming into his motorhome and, in a short bit of time, he would have it cleaned out, discarding anything that was soaked. He did think of drips that might occur between the motorhome and the Range Rover and parked immediately next to the door, sliding the body effortlessly across the floor and into the back. Peter stuffed a small nylon bag with drugs and paraphernalia and slid Klaus's passport and five thousand dollars in cash in the back pocket of the jeans. He left the body near the border south of San Diego, knowing the news would report it as a drug murder—just another drug murder. The local news covered the discovery late that night and, as predicted, assumed a connection between the German tourists disappearing in Tijuana and the almost decapitated body found near Brown Field.

ℰↃℰↃ

It wasn't arrogance as much as simple confidence that assured Peter he would never be caught. The family would not cooperate with a local investigation. Rather, they would conduct their own. If they ever did find out the truth, they would never report it. There was too much at stake for a local jurisdiction to hand out some criminal penalty. If they wanted, they could have the perpetrator tortured, killed, whatever they liked. Local police got snoopy and asked the wrong questions, especially when the very rich were involved. They needed privacy more than they needed local justice.

This would hurt, though. Klaus was a named heir— an heir in training and being groomed to carry on in exactly the same manner—and it would severely set back the family's plans. There would not be just another one of those funerals. Everyone would show up for this one. Everyone. It wouldn't be in some family chapel with the retired priest presiding. The local Bishop would insist on the family using his cathedral and he would personally preside. This was what a male heir got. This one would require the best security the German government could provide because simply everyone would be there.

CHAPTER 27

The priest answered his phone as he sat poolside, sipping a cold beer. It was Armand Schultz. He never had any kind of salutation to offer, he would just begin talking. The priest listened quietly as Armand detailed forensic evidence and eye witness accounts of a young man who visited his granddaughter during a dinner party and then stayed overnight.

The young man was introduced as a cousin to some of the guests, but others were simply told he was a friend of the family. The only cousin in the United States would be a very distant cousin whose family lived in New York. By all accounts, the description of the young man fit that of Peter exactly.

Peter's family offered Peter's DNA to Armand and his investigators with the assurance no police would be involved.

"We have an agreement that, if certain conditions are met, the two families can handle the matter quietly."

"Have you decided on an option?"

"I don't want to see the young man's family suffer as we have, that would not be kind, so I have probably—and

I say probably—eliminated the option of eye for an eye. He can live. Maybe."

"I see."

"He might prove useful, as you have proven to be most useful and loyal. As Martin has proven useful. As you know, once one takes a life, the horrible shock of that is past and a second event is not as traumatic, and the third is less so. Would you not agree?"

"Absolutely, sir, especially when an event would prove to further a righteous cause."

"Exactly. Now, this is something we may want to consider as we approach this young man. Of course, not just anyone can approach him and advise him of the decisions that have been made regarding the rest of his life. And so I turn to you. You know the art of persuasion."

"In its many forms, sir."

"Of course, the young man may think by ignoring us, evading us, or even worse, defying us, he will be able to get away. He may even desire to go to the police in the hopes of finding another way out of this, but I can assure you, the police in that locale would fully cooperative with us. They would even appreciate that we have kept this a quiet family matter and do not need to use their resources. Going to the police is not an option here. Complying with our plan is the only option. Can you appreciate that?"

"Absolutely, sir."

"I am aware this young man is wandering around in a motorhome and, once we have decided on a comprehensive plan for him, we will identify his whereabouts and I will send you further instructions."

"I am at your service, sir."

The priest sat back and reflected for a minute, then looked at his watch. Twenty minutes to five on a Saturday afternoon. He had established a custom of praying

Sunday Vespers in the church, and the first Vespers of
Sunday he set for five in the evening every Saturday. Few
people ever came, but there were regulars, especially
when the really devout Americans came down for the
winter. The locals had never been taught the daily prayer
of the church and had no real appreciation for it. But the
wealthy, devout Americans liked this refined touch and,
instead of a few pesos clinking in the basket, there was
always the soft sound of the paper bills they gave. The
priest dressed quickly in his black shirt and white collar
and walked slowly toward the church.

CHAPTER 28

Grady enjoyed the heat of a Seattle summer, lamenting it never lasted long enough. The old deck was gone and he was up early, excavating for the cement pads to support the new one. He had scheduled a concrete pour the next morning and, by noon, was finished setting all of the forms. As he washed his hands in the garage sink, Jimmy rolled slowly into the driveway in the government-issued Pontiac. They walked to the back yard to inspect the work.

"This gal of yours, Melissa Eggers. Interesting background. She gets axed by MIT and ends up with a top-secret security clearance and is contracting with a marine colonel in San Diego, doing his investigative legwork around NCIS. There's something here. I checked on her security status and that set off alarms all over the place, and I just sit back and see who jumps where. The colonel's CO is the one who jumped the highest. I traced some calls to and from his office, and lordy, lordy, what did I find. The check from Northwestern cleared though a company in Carlsbad, California, and guess who owns it. This young lady's father. Funny thing is, he owns a few other companies, one of which recovers stolen military weapons. This one looks like a deep cesspool. You got our attention, buddy. What's your interest in this thing?"

"Not sure I have any. I was brought in to investigate the theft of personal funds over the Internet and the CEO isn't interested in what I found. I have a piece of code written by this woman that sits on a server like a time bomb and then delivers, at will, names, account numbers, passwords, anything it wants, and no one seems the least bit interested but you guys. Hey, I'm submitting a bill and then I'm out of it."

Jimmy walked down the embankment in his fifty-dollar dress shoes to inspect the forms. He looked across the yard into his own. "Probably about time for me to get my own deck done." He tapped the forms and kicked a few rocks. "I want this one for myself. If I pass this over to the geeks in my office, someone else is going to run with this and probably in the wrong direction for a long time. I need you, usual arrangements, to pick up where you left off with Northwestern. You'll talk to me and me alone. I'll take whatever heat it generates."

"Damn, Jimmy, I was hoping to get my deck done while the sun's out and move the hell out of this slum by fall."

"God and country call you, young man. God and country."

"What access do I get?"

"I'll give you what I can and still keep my job."

∽∾∽

The first thing Jimmy wanted to know was what Melissa was doing for the colonel. Grady would have a cover, something about the FBI audit of security clear-ances Jimmy had started already. Now they would focus on the geeks doing business for the Department of Defense and Grady was doing deep background on randomly selected contractors. It would be more a skills assessment and then compliance with NISCAP and NISP. It just so happened that Melissa Eggers had been randomly selected for this audit.

San Diego was a Navy town. After that, there was surfing, some bio-tech research, and now drug trafficking. Grady sat in the ground-floor bar of the Holiday Inn, watching the local late news. A body of a German tourist had been found nearly decapitated in the south bay area of San Diego County, near the border. The bartender shrugged. He mumbled something about legalizing drugs to get rid of the drug lords. Grady smiled and sipped his beer. Another patron argued something about legalizing drugs being the dumbest thing he ever heard of and bartender refilled his drink for free. Within minutes, the story was forgotten and everyone watched footage of the arrival of another carrier returning to port, families reunited, and fathers holding their babies for the first time.

When the weather segment started, a tall fit marine colonel approached Grady, his right hand extended. "Grady Marcs?" Grady nodded. "Colonel Jerry Bartle. Sorry about meeting in this dive bar, but my CO didn't want us to meet on base and this was on the way home."

෴

Bartle told Grady about the work Melissa did for him on the base and nothing more. He did not detail any of the results of her findings, just that she did some contract investigative work, allowing him to circumvent the normal red tape and political bullshit anyone with rank in the United States military encountered on a daily basis. He was hoping this would get a gentleman's pat on the back

from Grady and the conversation would be over. Hire a
pretty gal to come in and get your job done faster and
more effectively—what military guy wouldn't appreciate
that?

Grady usually didn't like career military types, especially the ones who could not remember if they had fired
a weapon in hostility or not, which meant they had not.
They got behind a desk and kissed enough ass to get to
ever bigger desks with better views and more pretty
things on their chests. Just being in theater usually got
them up the ranks nowadays, so Bartle's foot-on-the-
ground experience in two Iraqi wars got him the birds.
No kills, just effective orders in lopsided wars where the
outcome was inevitable and well known before they ever
started. He would have enjoyed a beer with the marines
walking off the carrier, much more than this inflated, lying desk jockey.

Grady asked about any known associations off the
base that might bring into question her loyalty or her real
agenda in providing investigative work to the marines.
Bartle lied, claiming she worked alone. The business between his CO and Melissa's father was none of his concern and even less this former ranger. Grady persisted
with some questions about results of her efforts and
Bartle held up his hand. It was all top secret and no civilian who just blew into San Diego was going to tap into
that. If the brass in DC wanted answers, they would be
out there asking themselves and, until then, secrets would
remain just that. Bartle held his hand out to shake, and
Grady smiled, walking out of the bar.

Grady knew these types well. Bartle would tell
Melissa of the conversation they had in the bar and knew
she would begin looking into his background. What she
would find was a well-written history meant to obscure
the truth of Grady's true skills and background. She

would be directed to a honey pot of information, some legitimate, most completely fabricated, but ostensibly hidden behind a secure firewall that she would have to breach. Once she breached the security measures, they would then have leverage, if needed, when they sat and talked with her.

Grady walked by the Maritime Museum, admiring the tall masts and workmanship of the sailing vessels tied to the pier. The black Lexus RX rolling slowly behind him two blocks away, with no lights, was an obvious tail. He guessed it was Bartle, but that Lexus was a pretty nice vehicle for his pay grade. Maybe it was the CO, Brigadier General Malcom Durning. Now there was a war hero. He fought his way up the ladder, both on the field and internally. No one walked away unscathed after tangling with him and their victories were always short lived, with a few rare exceptions. He and Mark Burgess had a run in over field supplies once. Mark won and got the supplies he needed and Durning had to wait. Grady doubted Durning knew he had served under Mark, but it would be worth seeing the look on his face.

 හⓈහ

Brigadier General Malcom Durning was busy all morning, but was always happy to help out the FBI or anyone legitimately interested in securing our nation's borders. His secretary suggested dinner at Donovan's downtown. There would be a standing reservation in the general's name. It would be business casual.

 හⓈහ

Durning was a tall, strikingly fit, handsome, and charismatic man with a painful grip. Grady gripped back harder and saw the general's eyes cloud over. Grady liked steak houses but, from the looks of the clientele, he wondered if he wasn't in for an over-cooked piece of gristle. It wasn't his crowd—mostly bankers and lawyers. He ordered a double Canadian Club on the rocks while the general took his standing order of Bourbon, with delight. The general acknowledged several people, standing, gripping, grinning, and sitting again until the next schmuck came along, wanting to shake his hand.

Grady passed on the seafood appetizers, eating some bread instead. "As you know, General, the FBI has asked me to do some back ground checks, pretty randomly I think, on security contractors. Just some routine look-see, I think. You know the woman I am here to ask about, Melissa Eggers?"

"Yeah. My colonel uses her. He gets around NCIS and operates pretty independently. Nothing huge, just some petty stuff that I don't want to be bothered with. Seems to like her. He referred her to some pal of his in New York, Wall Street geek type who has a problem. I understand she's good and has been back there helping out."

Grady smiled to himself. There was a reason the general was giving her up so easily. This wasn't orders from above. There wasn't much above this brigadier general. He was trading.

"I understand you have worked with her father?"

"Yep, a decent citizen. He has a knack for recovering lost armaments. I say lost, but I was in supply long enough to know they were usually stolen."

"And often recovered by the very people who stole them."

"Maybe, but I get them back."

"So we pay for the same bullets twice."

"Better that than being hit by them once." He wasn't

smiling. This was the deal. He would give up the daughter if Grady would send the signal back up the chain to leave the father alone. "You were a ranger. Front line, I understand. You know what it means to be shot at, and the more I can do to get weapons back into the right hands, the more securely I sleep. I don't know what the hell this gal really does or doesn't do. I was given Bartle and told him I wanted results on information leaks. And he seems to have stopped them. But I've got my own fights, bigger fights, and if this gal is dirty, I don't want to know. I just want her gone, and maybe Bartle will go with her." The general cut into his steak. "You probably know Bartle never saw a day of combat in his career and he sits on his fat ass drinking out of that titanium coffee mug like he runs the Marine Corps."

Grady did not ask any further questions, except for the contact name in New York, and was told to call the general's secretary in the morning and he would have it. They finished dinner, sharing stories about Afghanistan, Colonel Mark Burgess, and how Mark screwed the general good. They both felt it was too goddam bad he was out of the service because the country needed patriots like him and the general wanted the chance to get even.

As they finished, the general gracefully pulled an envelope from the breast pocket of his jacket. "Like I said, I want to keep the old man in operation, but these are his cronies. They are not known for being kind and delicate to anyone who they think is putting their livelihood at risk. Watch yourself around them. Vietnam special forces. They might be getting old but, as you know, some things you just don't forget."

CHAPTER 29

It cost a lot of money to retrieve the body from Mexico, but not nearly as much if the ambulance drivers had not slipped across the border out of the United States while transporting it. Mexican officials saw things differently. They made it easier to do business. The body they delivered for the autopsy looked similar, but no one that night really knew who it was or how long that body had actually been dead. It would all take a few days to sort out and the body of Klaus would already be laid out in a cool, clean laboratory.

The priest had just settled in from the first funeral in Germany and he was on the phone preparing to go again. Armand Schultz called and told him it would not be necessary to come. The local bishop agreed to officiate. The funeral would be held with an empty casket and only five of them would know. The Bishop would pray over an empty box while small bits of anything that could be found were being collected and catalogued from the body. The box would be burned and these hollow ashes set in their designated place in the family mausoleum. Later, once they were satisfied, they would place Klaus's body into the furnace, away from crying eyes, switch the ashes, and, only then, allow the body to rest in eternity, and they would have all the truth about his death they would ever need.

The forensics team was ordered again to go to Mexico and tell Armand what they found. They would easily and accurately reconstruct the last hours leading up to the death of Klaus and report to the five. The team left with their evidence for San Diego, by way of Mexico City.

Governments were often limited in what they could spend, even on the most secretive and important assassinations. Loyal subjects with intense patriotic feelings would do a very good job on these limited resources, but the very best came at a price. Depending on what the forensics team found, the response from the five would have many options, terminating one or several lives would be among the choices.

The evidence told them the same person who had killed Gretta also killed Klaus. They had written the true name of the young man and sealed it in their evidence file. The file was delivered by hand the next morning to Armand Schultz. He read each page carefully and knew immediately what he could and could not do.

It never made sense to execute blood feuds between families of means. This did not further the cause. Rather, it served only to destroy the fabric of both families. Low-level crime syndicates used blood feuds to instill fear and they were often manipulated for this very effect. Keep these lower level people fighting each other for meager control of petty prostitution and drug trafficking and they would never be organized enough to control the real money. It might even be beneficial to capitalize on the media confusion and blame one of the syndicate families for the death.

Once again, the five would decide in good time, after

Armand put the facts in front of them and their options
were completely considered. It might even be a good
thing to do nothing at all and simply remember Gretta
and Klaus as a fresh, smiling handsome young people and
let it go. The loss was painful to them, but it was wiser
not to let anyone know how really devastating it was to
the entire family.

On the other hand, if a member of another family
was actively attempting to minimize the influence of the
families as a whole, then all families would be interested
in a permanent solution and no one with vested interests
would object. It was important to project normalcy, to be
a family in mourning over the loss of a treasured son and
grandson, a named heir. Be there for all members, allow
the young and innocent to absorb it and learn from it, silence those who would talk too much about it. Convince
the world they were loved and would be greatly missed,
and their faith in God would hold them in good stead.
When it was time to act, those who knew them well
would understand they had considered the options carefully and would see the value and wisdom of whatever
choice they made. In the report, the name of Melissa Eggers appeared several times. She had met Klaus and she
would become aware he had gone missing. Knowledge of
the incident would need to be contained and the perpetrator detained in a civil, yet secure, manner until a final decision was made. Armand decided it was not time to ask
the priest not for his skills at saying a funeral mass, but to
resolve the problem. The priest took the call late at night,
his wife sleeping peacefully.

eↄeↄ

Father Enrique Gustavus rarely wore his black shirt
with the little white square showing at the Adams apple,

but always did when he needed to go to El Norte. He spoke passionately fluent California Baja Spanish, but it was not his native tongue. He was born in the Bronx and had served the Archdiocese of New York faithfully until he decided to get married. He had lived on the Schultz estate in Germany for almost two years with his beautiful wife until the more traditionalist elements in the Schultz family insisted on a celibate family priest. They retired him to the location of his choice and he chose the Baja Peninsula, building an expansive villa overlooking the tranquility of the bay at Mulege. The call from Armand Schultz with a specific request on the matter of Peter came at four in the morning and Father Gustavus was driving toward San Diego by six.

The twelve-hour drive along the often-treacherous highway passed easily as Father Gustavus listened to the New Testament being read in Russian, the newest of the fifteen languages he could speak. He presented his United States Passport at the border and was waved through with a courteous smile. He stopped at his rented mailbox and took the manila envelope out to his car. There were several pictures of Peter, the motorhome, the headless body, the blood on the carpet, the knife used, and many other items.

The actual nature of the favor he was asked to complete was left to some interpretation. It was clear the dead body was that of Klaus Dieter, and it was also clear Klaus had been murdered by Peter. He was not being asked to punish Peter, as had been the nature of previous favors asked by the Schultz patriarch. This seemed to be more spiritual in nature.

The specific request in writing in the envelope dealt with Peter's safety and the location of the motorhome, and ended with, *Please resolve this*. Very shortly after in the same note, *We will find a need for Peter in the future,* just as the Schultz family had found need for Father Gustavus.

And Martin.

Armand Schultz had used the word "resolve" when referring to the matter. The word had a softer, more forgiving tone to it and reflected Armand's feeling in the first conversation they had had about Peter.

Father Gustavus drove to the motorhome and found it parked on the street, a Lexus behind it. It had been moved from the woman's driveway.

"Peter?" Father Gustavus spoke with a loud, forced New York accent when he was in the United States, clearly identifying him as not Mexican. "Peter? I would like to talk with you." He pounded on the door.

Peter opened the door. "A priest. I think I recognize you—"

"Father Antonio Gustavus. I am a friend of the Schultz family and I met you several years ago when I worked on their estate in Germany. More recently, I think you attended a family event in Germany." He held out his massive hand for Peter to shake. "May I come in?"

"I remember you. Yes, please come in."

Father Gustavus sat at the table and opened the envelope, sliding the pictures out in a neat pile. "Why don't you look through those for a moment and then we'll talk?"

Peter scratched his wrists and then looked up at the priest. "What is there to say?"

"Not a lot. I want you to pack something, a few bags, and come with me to my home in Mexico. I think it would be best if you did not argue about this."

"How long will we be there?"

"I don't know. But it will be safer for you. You see, the body the police have is not Klaus Dieter and they are going to discover that in the next day or so. I am going to have someone come and drive this motorhome to a safe location. Leave the key in the ignition if you would."

e⁄ɔe⁄ɔ

They ate just before crossing the Mexican border, and then lightly as they gassed the Mercedes, and arrived hungry and tired at six the next morning in the driveway of the villa at Mulege. "You should call your father," Father Gustavus said as he showed Peter to his suite. "The pool and spa are out that way, the kitchen is down that hallway, and Martin will help fix you anything you may like to eat. My wife will come and go as her business dictates and I have some work to do. Otherwise, please make yourself at home."

Peter watched a variety of American, Mexican, and European television stations through most of the morning. He slept for a few hours and then walked out to the pool to lie in the sun. A young Caucasian man introduced himself as Martin, asked if he wanted a drink, and then made him a rum and coke. "I told Mrs. Gustavus you were out here and she is going to join you in a few minutes."

Elena Gustavus was a taller woman with dark red hair and a deep Irish accent. She sat on the edge of a chaise lounge and exchanged polite conversation with Peter, welcoming him to her home. She excused herself and Peter was again alone by the pool. His cell phone buzzed. It was his father.

"Peter, I understand you are safe. It was so tragic what happened to that young man Klaus Dieter. His grandfather is so distraught, but we spoke at some length last night. He said you would be safe there."

"Where am I?"

"You are with people who understand us and you can

consider yourself inside now and you will be well taken care of."

"Inside what?"

"Well, the family, of course." His father paused momentarily. "That nice young lady you brought to New York, I am sure she is a fine young woman, but she will never understand and it just does not make any sense to contact her right now, don't you think? I mean, this whole thing just needs to settle down, let the facts sort themselves out and we just move on. I think it would be best if you just stayed there for a while, maybe a couple of months. You're with good people."

Good people indeed. They would help the family in any way they could.

Their first dinner together was served in the formal dining room by Martin. "So you were able to speak with your father today." Father Gustavus slurped his wine.

Peter nodded slowly. "Yes, I did. He agreed I should stay with you for a while."

"Excellent, we will be happy to have you stay as long as you like."

Peter stared at him. "I don't want to impose—"

"Trust me, you are not imposing. We think of you as family."

"That's very nice of you to say. I may need to leave from time to time. I have a commitment—"

"No, there is no need to leave." Father Gustavus smiled. "No need at all."

"But, I have a commitment—"

Father Gustavus fought with a small bit of gristle on his steak, fingering it to his plate. "Peter, if you leave, I will find you and do to you exactly what you did to Klaus Dieter, and I will do it gladly and with your father's and grandfather's blessings. They know exactly why you are living here with me and have approved every action I take. You killed two members of the Schultz family. What did you think would happen to you? If you succeed in leaving or even attempt that without my permission, I am to send your head to the Schultz family in Germany and I will take your body out into the ocean and feed it piece by piece to the sharks." Father Gustavus filled his mouth with more steak. "You've done something that ordinarily would get you the death penalty. Staying here in Mulege is certainly better than that, no? You will leave when you are told you can leave."

Peter ate silently, staring at the priest. "What does his family want from me?"

"Want? That's an odd question considering you just killed two of their heirs." Father Gustavus poured more wine and offered to fill Peter's glass. Peter nodded. "The Schultz family—and your family, for that matter—don't want anything, ever. They own so much there is nothing left to want." Father Gustavus sipped loudly. "I am pretty sure there is an agreement now that you will need to do something for the Schultz family."

"I don't have any skills."

Father Gustavus laughed a deep, guttural laugh, looking over at his beautiful Irish wife. "No skills?" He set his glass down. "Let me ask you something. This boy, Klaus Dieter, is not the only person you have killed, is he? You killed that girl, their granddaughter, up in Santa Monica. No?" Father Gustavus laughed again. "Look, I know people. I also know what it feels like to kill. It's a magnificent sense of power. I love it."

Peter smiled. "Yes, I have to admit I did enjoy it, both times."

"No skills? People like you and me are rare and valuable to people like Armand Schultz." Father Gustavus pushed the empty plate away. Martin appeared and removed it from the table then poured more wine. "You have an inherent and useful skill, you just don't know anything about it. Your actions were crude and full of carelessness. Left to yourself to handle these matters, you would be lying on a table in a few years waiting for you jailer to inject and kill you. Yet out of this horrific affair, these ultimate insults and harm to one family, they see good in you." Father Gustavus sipped his wine. "To be honest with you, young man, I don't see anything useful yet. Anything."

CHAPTER 30

Melissa watched the motorhome roll quietly away as she parked in her driveway. She had called Peter several times and now even his voice mail was turned off. She decided not to fly to New York, but instead she would work remotely. She tried Brett's number, then reached Mark and he explained he would need Brett's approval for a remote connection, and promised to call her right back.

The knock at the front door surprised her a little. She did not recognize the man standing on the front porch. She opened the door slightly.

"Melissa? My name is Grady Marcs. I am with the FBI and would like to ask you some questions about your security clearance."

"Certainly. Can we do this some other time? I am in the middle of some work."

"I leave town tomorrow and I would like to finish up and not have to return, so now is better than later."

"Tonight, I can meet you tonight. There is a restaurant I like, at the Rancho Valentia Resort, not far from here. I can give you directions—"

"I'll find it. How about seven."

"Fine, fine. You won't mind if my father joins me, will you? I'll make the reservations."

"Good. I have some questions for him as well." The connection was set and she was free to work. Instead, she called Colonel Bartle. He had met Grady, yes, and it seemed all very routine. The general had met him, too. There didn't seem to be anything to worry about. The feds did this all the time.

∽∾∽∾

Grady hated the rich who felt compelled to flaunt their money. The resort parking lot was full of European luxury cars—a waste of money in any economy. He didn't think the men who were there really wanted to be there. It seemed more like a place women went to brag that they had been there. They went to show they could afford the forty-nine dollar steaks and then never ate the whole thing. The men looked sterile. Hired executives, mostly, with that pale, bland look of a yes-man. They did whatever the board told them to and this place was the reward for that. He sat at the bar and ordered a double Canadian Club on the rocks. The bartender didn't seem to fit with the pretty boys serving at the tables. And it was just pretty boys serving, no women.

He had arrived at fifteen to and figured he would be finished with the first drink by the time Melissa got there. By twenty after seven, he asked the host if she had made a reservation and she had, but was now late and they would need to give up the table. Grady went back to his second drink.

By the time he ordered his third drink, Melissa walked over to him at the bar and offered her hand. "Mr. Marcs, I am so sorry we are late. Something came up."

"I hope it was manageable."

"Well, we're about to be seated and we would love it—"

Grady placed some cash on the bar. "I'm not eating. I have two questions for you and your father can be handled by someone else."

Melissa stood, blinking, then smiled. "Well, there we go. What kind of questions do you have?"

"First, how do you know Gene Surrey?"

"Gene Surrey, let's see, I am almost ready to say I don't, but that name—"

"I hate liars Ms. Eggers."

Melissa played the coy and beautiful trophy well, just the type who would love to spend their petty little days in a resort like this. "Well, there you go again. You are just full of little surprises. Gene is a client and I do not share information about my confidential clients. I have done some technical consulting for him."

"Second question. Dr. David Rohr wants to know if you have used the code that got you expelled from MIT in the recent past." Grady slammed the last of the drink back and smiled. "Third question. Who are you working for in New York?"

Now she was angry. "Like I said, Mr. Marcs, my client list is confidential. And what does this have to do with my security clearance?"

"A lot. The FBI is interested in any false information you may have supplied when being vetted for your initial security clearance. Lying is not acceptable, and concealing information about being expelled from a university is considered lying." Grady finished his drink and started to walk away. "Well, I need to report my findings to the FBI and I will do so. I will tell them that you refuse to cooperate and they will need to decide if you keep your security clearance. You have a nice meal, Ms. Eggers."

Grady had seen all he needed to see.

൭උൈ

Chin and Boyle joined them at the table. Melissa and her father greeted them with broad smiles.

"Find out who he really is." Arthur Seward placed on envelope on the table. "Find his family and start with one of them. In my forty years of having a security clearance, I have never been investigated by anyone like him. Something else is going on." He turned to his daughter. "Now, Melissa, if you're involved in anything other than the type of business we have always done, you need to tell me. I need to know."

The coy and beautiful trophy kissed her daddy's cheek and ordered the filet mignon.

൭උൈ

Melissa dialed Peter's number and he answered. She asked where he was and what happened to the motorhome and he didn't answer. He said he was busy now with something else. No, she could not come to where he was. No, he was not in New York. Something very important had come up and he needed to focus on that. And, no, he didn't care what she had done or planned to do, he would never tell anyone. He had no business telling anyone, and he might be implicated also. No, he was not under investigation or cooperating with police on any investigation. Don't worry.

"You got in where you wanted to be and you need to finish this from here on, on your own. I can no longer help you." Peter ended the call and Melissa stood in her living room staring out at the street.

This new thing changed it all. Destroying the computing systems used in securities transactions and storing financial data was certainly something she was able to do, but what would be the ultimate effect? Would it destroy the rich? Not likely. It was nonsense to think she could destroy the rich. Peter had that right. It would be better to disrupt their lives, systematic disruption, taking money from them here then there, maybe causing the market to implode on itself. People would cause the markets to fail when they lost all confidence in it. Unexplainable disruptions and untraceable thefts. But it was still all about one family.

She set the parameters in the program for routine yet random search-and-destroy and search-and-transfer missions. Select an account, destroy it, or just transfer the funds out of it, leave no record of any kind and then sit for a random amount of time until another account was selected, fleeced, or destroyed. One day it might be the account of an old woman with fifteen thousand dollars and another day it might be an institutional account with fifteen billion dollars gone missing.

She would find the benign program and reveal it for an amateurs work and even trace it back to one of the people on the forums. Her own program would sit idle for three months and she would be long out of the system having solved their security problem and back to work for Colonel Bartle.

She had advised Brett and Mark to plan on rebuilding the servers. Better than using the same servers, buy new ones and start over. Don't cut corners. Don't take chances. They did as she advised and she was three thousand miles away with no remote access when they did it. Her program sat on Brett's computer until two days before execution and it found a nice cozy spot in the root directory. The timer was set for the first mission. Melissa had an inherent ability to wait as long as it took.

CHAPTER 31

Jimmy Steele sat on the new deck overlooking Lake Washington. It was hot for Labor Day, pushing the mid-nineties and that was hot for Seattle, period. "And you're going to leave this?"

"No time soon, that's for sure. Had the open house yesterday and three people showed up. Got an offer for fifty K below asking. Not interested. I can live here as long as it takes for the market to come back."

"You and I may be long dead from old age before that is likely to happen. You sold the Jackson Hole cabin I hear."

"Yeah, it sold pretty quick. I think we're going to rent a place in Steamboat for January and ski there this year. Grady Junior is signed up for some online home school option and that frees us up to get out of here before Christmas."

"Online high school? You sure?"

"We looked into it. I like the curriculum. And it's just for the break."

"What about college, is any good college going to take a diploma from an online school?"

"Average SAT score for the graduating class last year was eleven hundred. And, Jimmy, calm down. It's just for the break."

There was a pause. "That girl, Melissa Eggers. Nothing more about her?"

"Nada. You find anything?"

"Just that Arthur is not her real father. Mr. Eggers blew himself up, too much Vietnam on the brain. Mr. Eggers saved Arthur's life not in Vietnam, but after when the girl was only four or five—something about a botched drug run. He took out twenty Columbians and they got their asses out of there. Then he cracked, like when the girl was five, and the mother went boo boos into an institution somewhere, and Arthur took her in and adopted her."

"And her profile says she's capable of lying, hiding in the tall grass, waiting, and capitalizing on the best opportunities."

"Yes, sir, and that's what she is doing. Hiding in the tall grass in plain sight."

"Did you ever find out who she was working for in New York?"

"It's an odd connection. She was introduced to some people who manage the computing infrastructure for the New York Stock Exchange. She helped catch some hackers and they think she is a goddess. She had total access."

"You got someone on that?"

"Yeah. You. I had to walk this thing down the hall in DC myself and that's what has taken so god damn long to get back to you, but I got clearance to have you follow up. They agreed our geeks are good, but we need someone who already knows this gal."

"Domestic terrorism of our financial systems."

"That's what it looks like to me. If we give it to the in house geeks, they'll be looking for Muslims for the next two years. I want you to get her before she stands up in the grass. She's getting ready to do something and I would like to get this one before it happens for once."

೭ン೭ン

They were too late. While it appeared to be a common malfunction of the midnight differential backup, when employees at the Seattle-based investment company, Reed and Roe, readied themselves for the opening of the market to execute orders from clients, they had no funds. The market opened in a typical frenzy and orders were placed, but nothing would be considered a real trade until funds were in place to cover the orders. Every client account had been emptied. At close of business the previous day, the accounts balanced at exactly $348,567,456.32. Now there was nothing. There was not a single client showing assets of any sort. Sean Goode, the senior trader and adviser, whose client portfolio had the previous day boasted a value of $145,456,912.34, collapsed and died instantly when his oldest and most faithful client called to ask why his online account was showing a zero balance.

Reed and Roe was a small investment management firm, by all standards. Their requirements for account setup was a minimum of one million dollars and, while they did not have a wealthiest and most prestigious clients in the Pacific Northwest, they had some of the most faithful. One hundred percent of the client base was accepted into the asset management program by personal referral—no amateur day traders or laundered mob money. It was understood that most young clients signed on as a result of receiving inheritances and most were also professionally employed.

The partners, Nick Reed and Grant Roe, held an annual Christmas, not holiday, party for employees and clients and their immediate families. They gave individual gifts to each family.

Now, there were no assets. Reed and Roe was technically broke, all of their client's assets had disappeared, and they had no answers.

At noon, Melissa restored the assets. All of it except for the assets belonging to a client by the name of Stephan Heimlich. She didn't know why she picked this one, but she did. She told herself the guy was an asshole and deserved it. She would move his five and a half million dollars in assets around for a while, dispersing them into a variety of accounts. Melissa did not know of the fate of Sean Goode, but guessed the chaos and fear running through the veins at Reed and Roe would have somehow been delightfully entertaining. She guessed Stephan Heimlich would be told that his account was insured for five hundred thousand dollars and he would want an immediate explanation and the partners at Reed and Roe would not have any. They would have lost most of a tepid trading day and, at least, their losses were minimized by that fact, but they had to contend with the fact that one of their clients lost over five million dollars and they had no explanation.

The partners of Reed and Roe instructed their employees to call every one of their clients and explain that a computer malfunction had caused the temporary problem and their information security experts were tracking down the cause to ensure this would never happen again. Stephan Heimlich arrived at Reed and Roe with his complete portfolio and only then learned of the death of his adviser, Sean Goode. He expressed his sympathies and demanded an immediate meeting with the partners for an explanation.

The markets closed at one and the traders sat back in

their chairs, cursing silently, as they called each of their clients, many of them nursing chest pains and headaches. It was all over by four in the afternoon, except for the meeting taking place between the partners, Stephan Heimlich, the accountants, and the chief technology officer. This resulted in no answers. Stephan Heimlich left in a rage and called the police from his car.

The chief technology officer asked for a private meeting with Nick Reed and Grant Roe and explained they did know what happened to the money, but there were no traces of who had done it or where the money had ultimately ended up. It was flat-out stolen and they had no evidence. He explained that it could even have been an inside job.

The Seattle police did not have sufficient resources for this type of computer-based crime and, after taking Stephan Heimlich's statement, called the offices of Reed and Roe. They asked if they could interview the partners to begin their investigation, which would probably end up at the Seattle office of the FBI.

The disappearance of over three hundred million dollars, even temporarily, set in motion a news cycle that focused on the victims. Grady sat down with a short, neat scotch to watch some local news before the baseball game and frowned as one victim after another described their trading day. She had begun.

CHAPTER 32

Late summer was not typically the time to visit Mulege. Most ex-pats lived there between Halloween and Memorial Day and, during the summer, migrated back to their homes in El Norte. The climate in the winter was ideal—warm, dry, and easy on the arthritis. In late summer, it was hot, humid, and not at all comfortable. Many good restaurants were closed and the town was left to the locals not able to travel to cooler climates to wait out the excessive heat.

Peter took up writing in the morning by the pool and, in the afternoons, wandered the beaches to find secluded coves. He had begun to feel strangely sexual, fantasizing about finding complete strangers skinny dipping in these secluded coves, and he would join them, climaxing in sexual trysts he could write about the next day. So far, all he found were old men fishing from the edge of the beaches, smoking hand rolled cigarettes, and drinking warm beer.

Father Gustavus did not have a computer in the house. He ranted for an hour about his theories on how he had been hacked and spied on whenever he owned a computer and banned them from his home. He had a portable Olivetti typewriter for Peter to use. The writing was slow and tedious. There were too many errors in his typing to simply white out and type over, so he found himself retyping some pages three or four times. He decided the ten pages he had written so far would become a diary detailing his daily visits to the ocean and the sensuous young people he would meet there, even if he had to make up the encounters.

The jeep he was allowed to use did not run well. Until it warmed up, it would stall several times, and then, once it was warm, it would overheat. He ventured farther and farther down the beach each time he went out, hiking down steep, rocky slopes and, finding no sand or shade, crawled back up to the jeep and waited until he could start the jeep again and return to the house.

Father Gustavus believed in penance and redemption, and part of that was enduring the worst heat the Mexican sun could throw at him. The house had no air conditioning, and, when Peter would return, he would be sweaty, dirty, and barely able to move. After diving into the pool, he would try to find relief from the heat in a shaded corner, hoping for a cooling breeze that never came. Relief would finally come as the sun tucked behind the trees. A late afternoon snack would be served and they would talk.

∽∾∽∾

Father Gustavus had entered the Society of Jesus later in life than most men did. He was thirty when he made his initial application and it took over a year to complete the battery of psychological evaluations and interpersonal interviews. Up until he adopted the name Antonio Gustavus at the age of twenty-nine, he was known to his family and friends as Howard Nachman. At fourteen, he joined the Jewish Defense League, volunteered in the Israeli army, and finally worked for two years for Mossad. He could have spent his career in Mossad, but he knew he would always be a civil servant and never wealthy. The path he chose in the end allowed him to carry out the work he loved and to be richly rewarded for it. From this past life, he carried the tools necessary for survival.

Peter was convinced to join Father Gustavus as a volunteer at the mission church. A group of college students from Michigan were staying there, making necessary repairs to the buildings and helping with cleaning up a day care center so it could be used once again. "It will be like a favor in God's eyes for you to help these, his less fortunate people."

To say Father Gustavus was lecherous would have diminished the intensity of his interest in the young ladies from Michigan State University. Peter grasped for a word and could only think "lascivious." He had learned the word from his father, who had used it to describe his own paternal uncle and his groping of the young men and women who worked for him. Peter was not surprised to see this in Father Gustavus.

Father Gustavus actually enjoyed it. His leering and guttural laugh when he talked to the young women stopped just short of any physical contact. The women, as a group, would move away from him to a safe corner of the mission until he left.

This was someone Peter could trust. They ate dinner that night without Elena and Martin left after setting everything out on the side board.

"You like those college girls."

Father Gustavus looked up quickly, sharp eyed, and then smiled, his big menacing teeth showing. "Yes, I do. You noticed. I know well enough what I can do and what

I cannot do, but you will never tell me I cannot look. They are ravishing."

Peter ate silently for a few moments. "The guys are not bad either, wouldn't you agree?"

Father Gustavus shrugged. "I suppose, but you know there is nothing more cliché than a homosexual priest lusting after young men. If you like them, you can have them."

Peter stared for a long time at the large, bearded priest who chewed with his mouth open and slurped his wine. "You are a very sinful man. How do you expect God to forgive you?"

"God forgives everything. God is all love. All I need to do is confess my sins and God forgives me."

"Don't you have to show some sign of repentance, some desire to become a better person?"

Father Gustavus snorted as he laughed. "You are indeed a young man. You won't change. You will go on sinning your entire life, this sin, that sin, and then a new sin, and you will never stop. I am the vehicle God uses for you to admit you are a sinner and to seek his forgiveness and He grants it immediately."

"But what if you do something illegal?"

"That has nothing to do with sinning. If you are caught by the police, they will send you to jail. The trick is, young man, if you are going to do something sinful and it is also illegal, don't get caught. God will always forgive you, the people may not."

Peter sat back in his chair, looking puzzled. Father Gustavus nodded. "Michael Jackson was accused of molesting children and look at how many people cried so tearfully at the news of his death. They loved him anyway. Now, the pope, a brilliant scholar and a holy man, is discovered to have been a member of the Hitler Youth and no one forgives him. They curse him. Why do you think that is?"

Peter shrugged and shook his head.

"Well, I don't know either. I just know that if you sin, and it is illegal, you need to avoid the people if they don't like you."

Peter reflected for a moment. "Let me ask you something. Can something be illegal and not sinful?"

"Oh yes, very much so." Father Gustavus picked a piece of meat from between his teeth with a fingernail. "And we who believe in the afterlife are more concerned about this scenario than we are of the opposite, where something maybe legal but considered very sinful, aren't we?"

"Aren't they the same?"

"Ah, you have not given this much thought, have you?" Father Gustavus pushed his plate away. "What is a sin? Isn't it an intentional and willful desire to violate God's laws. Intentional and willful. I think most people who confess their sins to me have not sinned at all. Most of what I hear is human nature playing itself out. Take the young man who recently confessed to me he stole a loaf of bread. Now, the local police might want to slap him around a bit, and if he has done this sort of thing before, they may even put him in jail for a while as a petty thief, but in God's eyes, there is so much to consider before calling him a sinner. Was he poor and hungry? Did his mother beg him to do it? Did someone force or dare him to do it? Did he do it just to see if he could get away with it? I don't know, unless perhaps the penitent tells me these circumstances. What I have never heard, and I am still waiting to hear, is someone admit they did something to piss off God. Just to spite and disobey God. I have never heard that and I doubt I ever will."

Father Gustavus took a pear from the fruit bowl. "Let

me ask you this. When you cut that young man's head off, did you stop and consider why you were doing it? Did you consciously tell yourself you knew this was wrong, it offended God and all of humanity, and you chose to do it precisely because it was wrong and offended God?"

"Of course not. I just did it."

"Exactly. Now, we need to make sure the law never finds out what you did, and that is partly my job. But my point here, Peter, is do you think you committed a sin?"

"I don't believe in the concept of sin. I do not believe in God, the devil, heaven, hell, or anything like that. How could I have sinned?"

"Oh, young Peter." Father Gustavus shook his head. "It is very possible to sin, don't kid yourself. I will pray for you." He stood and pushed his chair back to the table. "But now I need to go. I will be back in a few days. Elena will be around off and on, Martin will be in tomorrow to clean. Just tell him what you like to eat, as usual. We will continue this discussion when I return. And, while I am away, maybe tomorrow or the next day, the college kids said they wanted to come up and use the pool. I know they would not want me around." He laughed deep and coarsely. "So please be a good host to them."

❦❦❦

Peter liked the one in the blue shorts. His strong, lean body presented many challenges. He was able to easily pick up any one of the girls over his head and toss her into the pool. Screaming. He made them scream. Peter learned his name was Chip. What an odd name to give to someone when Chip was born in the late eighties. It was such a fifties kind of name. He wondered if Chip's parents weren't a lot older when they had him. Maybe it was the father's name. He thought of Chip's bedroom at home. It would have sports posters, some odd books, a small desk, and trophies on the window sill. His clothes would be neatly folded and properly sorted in a small dresser, the loving touches of a mother who dearly missed her college boy.

The food came and went and Peter started to encourage the group to think about going back to the mission by ten. He used the excuse that he needed to get up early and drive south along the beach to find a place he had been told about where the locals went skinny dipping. He described it as a shaded area with a natural diving cliff. Chip and one of the other guys said they wanted to go. Peter smiled and felt inside the front of his shorts.

None of them were drunk but they insisted on hugging Peter and then each other, thanking him for such a wonderful time.

A tingling went through Peter's head as he hugged Chip. He patted the man on the back. "You guys aren't afraid of being kidnapped, I'm sure, with Chip here to protect you."

The girls laughed nervously. The other guys didn't really pay attention.

"Don't lose this guy." Peter patted Chip on the back again and decided Chip would be the next one.

CHAPTER 33

Grady stepped out of the cab into the thick, sultry New York afternoon. He was sweating immediately. He would take August in Afghanistan any day over the humidity of New York. The front office was cool and dry, but the server room was exactly like the street. Fans roared, but had little effect. Nate was sitting in surfer shorts with no shirt, trying to update security patches, sweat running freely down his back.

"We get a lot of security experts in here, and every time they tell me the place needs to be air conditioned and every time I put out a cup and I write 'air conditioning fund,' I get shit from you guys. I get told the New York Stock Exchange is the most envied stock market in the world, it is the model of free enterprise at its best, and it is also the most secure repository of investor information and securities in the world and any day these servers are going to crap out and shut the whole damn system down."

Grady smiled. "You should learn to speak your mind, friend, it does a man no good to hold back his opinions." He grabbed his shirt away from his skin, trying to allow the fans to cool him down, but to no avail. "You should air condition this room." He laughed.

"Sorry, it's so damn hot in here." Nate held out his hand. "Brett told me you would be coming. I didn't hear him let you in. I thought it was him standing there and, well…"

"Yeah, just another security expert. You know why I'm here."

"Yeah, the thing in Seattle, that thing with Reed and Roe. Not sure what that has to do with us. Our servers were definitely in the pathway, but the secure area network where they house their data is in Colorado somewhere and, once they update our databases with their trades, they are immediately routed to the SAN. We don't hold their data for any length of time. Trades are recorded and we never see or hold any financial records for their clients, ever."

Grady asked if Nate knew Melissa Eggers and he shrugged. "She caught those guys, but I think we would have caught them ourselves. Our perimeter security is very good. Those guys downstairs do a damn fine job."

Grady went to the white board and drew a diagram of Melissa's "Banker's Delight."

Nate smiled. "You think she planted this on my server? I'm not sure when she would've had the opportunity to install that. I just tossed the servers last week. She was cut off then from remote access and we degaussed the system over the weekend."

"Did she ever tell you how she cracked the grading system at MIT? The program was dormant on a connected workstation and was activated by the internal clock system and, bingo, one day after a complete scan of the system had been completed, it found the grading database and gave her administrative access from a remote computer that was never traced. That program is a mild version of this 'Bankers Delight.' I need to prove she loaded it up here, and to do that, I need to find it first."

"We check constantly for viruses, spy bots, root kits, and I have never found anything on the servers. There is a desktop support division under Brett and they are pretty sharp people. They check the same thing on a constant basis. Brett told me to give you free access to anything, so if you want to run your own scans, I set up an admin account for you both on the domain servers as well as the local workstations. You can remote in to any of one of them from here."

"I'm not going to find it that way. She's too good."

The log detailing all remote access to the system was well maintained and showed the IP and MAC addresses from which Melissa last remotely accessed the system. Nate provided a copy of the log. Grady called Jimmy Steele and was en route to Kennedy airport within the hour, catching the five o'clock direct flight to San Diego.

ℰᴔℰᴔ

The approach to Lindbergh Field required a low pass by the skyscrapers of downtown San Diego, many of the buildings to the left of the flight pattern higher than the landing path. Grady wondered what people who had never been to San Diego before thought of this after 9/11—a large commercial jet flying through a heavily populated downtown at eye level with many of the building occupants. Special Agent Jimmy Steele was waiting for him at the gate. "Let's go out the back steps. I've got a car just outside here."

All Jimmy could get was the IP and MAC addresses associated with Melissa's Internet service provider and they did not match the log. The addresses in the log were not associated with any public domain, which meant to

Grady it was a secure, exclusive domain, probably corporate or government. Jimmy's assistant special agent from Seattle was serving a warrant on the entity that governed and controlled IP addresses to determine who owned the one in the log. The car stopped a block down from Melissa's house.

"That's her father. He's been around all day. The other car belongs to a business associate of the father's."

"They're recovering stolen weapons for General Durning. They actually steal them, sell them, and then recover them. Everyone knows what's going on. They just can't stop the stealing." Grady closed the file. "I know the computer she's using and I know how she is masking the source computer. I will bet you the IP address belongs to the marines, and, when she is doing goodie-two-shoes security work for this guy, Colonel Bartle, he's so clueless he has no idea she is hijacking his system. I need to talk to the general, and you should be there because we may need some DC power to convince the general to co-operate. I'll bet he's still at dinner."

❧❧❧

They found General Durning at his table at Donovan's waiting for his desert. His party of four admirals, all dressed in civilian clothes, did not appear to enjoy the interruption. Jimmy convinced the general to join them briefly in the bar and Grady explained his theory. The general wanted him to work with NCIS, but Grady convinced him that he would, only if he could get to the system immediately and the NCIS investigators could be brought up to speed. The general seemed to understand the importance of the request, but insisted on ending his dinner party before he acted.

Grady and Jimmy waited in the bar. Grady's cell

phone rang. It was Mark. The servers had ceased func-
tioning and not because of the heat. He was in the middle
of the nightly backup and something interrupted the
queue. And then the systems just shut down. He tried to
reboot four or five times and immediately switched over
to the hot backup system and completed the off-source
backup of the day's trading activities. No one could determine if any data had been corrupted in the process and
nothing certain would be determined until the next morning. Grady walked over to the general's table and explained what had just happened.

"And you are certain it's this girl, the one working
for Colonel Bartle."

"I am. I just don't have any evidence. I need to get
into the system now."

The admirals politely left, eyeing Grady and Jimmy.
General Durning called Colonel Bartle and ordered him
to meet at the colonel's office immediately.

εοεο

Colonel Bartle and Major Markum rose and rigidly
saluted the general as they entered the office. "At ease.
Colonel, this is Special Agent Jimmy Steele and a private
investigator, Grady Marcs. I learned you and Mr. Marcs
have already met and you did not cooperate with him before." The general stood with his hands behind his back.
"You will do so now. Anything these two men ask of
you, consider it a direct order from me for you to cooperate. And if I discover any complicity in any illegal activity, or if I find that you did not take necessary security
precautions with a civilian contractor, you will see jail
time. Am I clear?"

εοεο

Melissa had succeeded in not only interrupting the backup process for the transactions servers, but she had also emptied four major investment accounts, the largest belonging to a German investment bank. She had not stolen the money, just moved it temporarily, and then returned it.

She did not see the German banker kill himself when it was discovered their accounts were showing no funds. She also did not hear the German television announcer talk about a crisis on Wall Street. She did not see Brett clutching his chest and falling over. He would survive, but his position might not. She did not see Nate sweating in his underwear, trying to explain a problem he knew nothing about—this she could only imagine.

All Melissa could see was the icy cold mai tai and the luxurious shrimp cocktail in front of her with her doting farther at her side.

CHAPTER 34

Peter started the jeep. It lurched and sputtered for a while until it was warm and then seemed to run better than usual. He sat idling in front of the mission, waiting for Chip and the other volunteer to come out. Chip was alone. Peter smiled.

The sun was already hot and the bikini top did little to protect them. Peter drove toward the water and the breeze was somewhat cooler, but not enough to make the day comfortable. Peter stopped the jeep fifteen miles down the coast where the road began to deteriorate into a bad trail. They were just twenty feet from the water and here there was a small sandy beach.

Chip had talked the entire time about his girlfriend back in Michigan and how they had thought about getting married, but he believed they should wait. He also felt he should get approval from his pastor since his father was dead and he really had no one like that to talk with. The whole idea of the trip to Mexico was his because he wanted to make sure it was the right decision to get married, and he didn't want to see another marriage end up in divorce. His mother had warned him against going, being as there was so much violence in Mexico and so many people getting killed. He told her it was all about drugs and, since he didn't do drugs of any kind, no one would want anything to do with a poor volunteer at a small remote mission. She still objected and there wasn't anything he could do about that.

When Peter shut the engine off, Chip was quiet and Peter smiled. "Nice day for a swim."

Chip squinted from under his Michigan baseball cap as Peter walked naked from the jeep toward the water. Peter waded up to his hips and dove under. He emerged and looked back to see Chip leaning, crossed arms, against the jeep.

"Come on." Peter waved at him. Chip shook his head. Peter sighed. "What's wrong?"

"I don't like salt water. I almost drowned in the ocean when I was a kid."

Peter waved both arms at him. "Lame. Totally lame. How can you drown? It's not even three feet here." Drowning him would be a good way to do it. He wondered what it was like, taking in water until there was no chance of recovering, choking off the air. How far into the body did the water penetrate? "Fine, let's go back to the house and use the pool."

❧❧❧

Father Gustavus looked at the body of the young naked man floating face down in the pool. Peter sat at the table, typing slowly and rhythmically. Father Gustavus walked around and stood by Peter, saying nothing. He went back inside the house and returned with Martin. "Peter, give us a hand here."

Peter looked up with genuine surprise. "Oh, certainly. Where shall we put him?"

"For now, we have an empty freezer. We'll put him in there. The people from the mission will start to ask. I won't know anything and you will need to go away for a while." The process was fairly simple and the freezer lid shut with a quiet thud. "Thank you, Martin. Now, Peter, we need to talk about something you need to do up in San Diego. First, you and I are going fishing."

ℰ✺ℰ✺

Martin cleaned the pool, scrubbed the deck around it, and looked several times for any sign Chip had ever been at the house. He defrosted the freezer, wiping the interior clean with bleach.

The students working at the Mission stopped at the house, asking for Chip, and Martin invited them in, pretending to call Father Gustavus, allowing them to wander through the house, and finally offering food or anything they wanted to drink. The girls sat by the pool, obviously distressed.

"Is he missing, this friend of yours?"

"He was supposed to meet up with Peter. I was supposed to go with them."

"How long has he been missing?"

"Just today. Where is Peter?"

"He left with Father Gustavus to do some fishing early this morning. When were you supposed to meet him?"

"This morning at nine or so. He left without me."

"Have you spoken with the police?"

"We tried, but the officers on duty did not speak English."

"I can help you. I speak fluent Spanish and I deal with the local police all the time. Do you want me to call? Or perhaps we can go to the station and speak directly with them." Martin stood quietly. "May I ask if your friend used recreational drugs? Do you know if he tried to purchase some here in Mexico?"

"What do drugs have to do with him going missing?"

"Well, it might explain all of this. Perhaps he felt he needed to hide from you, do something you might not approve of, and he'll make his way safely back. I see that a lot with guests who visit here in Mulege. They may feel shame over something they want to do while on vacation and they find a quiet, secret place, to—well, you know."

"What are you talking about?"

"People do many strange things when they are in a foreign country where they think no one sees what they are doing. Some come for the drugs, some for…well, sexual activity that they would otherwise not engage in among their peers. I would guess your group is leaving soon?"

"We drive out of here in two days."

"Yes, well, maybe he needed to experiment, try something new in these last few days. Often, when students go on spring break, a few will go missing and then turn up just hours before they are scheduled to depart, many with secrets they will never tell anyone. Whether it is drugs, or even something sexual, depending on the nature of the acts, the locals sometimes do not like what these guests get involved in. If it is drugs, then sometimes it's perceived they have money, and some criminal elements try to get that money, and you must have been warned about trying to do things like this alone, always travel in a group."

"You're saying he was kidnapped."

"Well, the majority of people who visit here in Mulege experience nothing but warm weather and great hospitality. There are others, however, who travel here for nefarious purposes and they do not always fare well.

We really should talk to the police and, if they ask you personal questions about your friend, they are only trying to determine if he was one of these people so they will know where to start looking. I suggest you tell them everything. This is not a time to hide secrets about your friend."

Martin knew well the police would look at this group of rich college kids and start to ask questions about drugs or hiring prostitutes, male and female. The college kids would be embarrassed and nervous, and at first would not cooperate, But then they would talk a bit, telling the police a few things, and the police would start to dismiss them as spoiled punks. They would take a report and start asking local contacts if the kid had been seen buying drugs or hanging out where the male prostitutes are. The college kids would tell the police about plans to meet with Peter, and the police would come to the house. Martin would welcome them, show them the itinerary for the fishing trip, and give them the contact information. The charter service would look up the itinerary and confirm Father Gustavus, a frequent client, had reserved the boat two days earlier, and he and a young man fitting Peter's description had arrived at the docks and left on the charter boat hours before Peter was supposed to have met with Chip. As far as the police would be concerned, this Chip guy was just another rich college kid trying to score some cheap drugs before he went back to the States. Martin called the charter service to make sure they had the correct time stamps on the documents.

≈≈≈

The boat motored overnight around the southern tip of the Baja Peninsula, stopping for fuel, and finally arriving in Ensenada early the next morning. Along the way, in the darkness of the Mexican night, Father Gustavus did to Chip what he had promised to do to Peter. He made Peter watch and was somewhat delighted that Peter showed no fear, remorse, or emotion.

"These sharks eat well along here," Father Gustavus said.

He ate a good breakfast and the two walked toward the storage garage where he kept a Lexus. He handed out ten dollar bills to the boys, who had just polished the car, and thanked them all.

"You need to be more careful, am I clear, Peter? You will be useful only if you are not as careless as you have been these past two days. We need to conduct some business in San Diego and you need to do exactly as you are told, am I clear?"

Peter nodded.

"Good, good."

Father Gustavus wondered what he would have to do to Peter when the business in San Diego was completed. If the boy could do the job, there might be a future for him in the family, but once the debt was repaid, there would be no requirement to keep him alive.

CHAPTER 35

The judge refused to issue a warrant for the arrest of Melissa Eggers. He cited a lack of sufficient evidence for his refusal and warned Jimmy Steele not to shop around for a judge. "Put something in front of me that will stick and you can have your warrant, otherwise stop this pre-emptive law enforcement."

Grady held the log of all of the IP addresses associated with her. He explained to the judge that none of them matched the IP from the logbooks. If she was masking the IP address, this would be very difficult to prove in the short term, and really not until they found the computer her efforts originated from. In time, he could find it, but she was active now and capable of inflicting great harm on the New York Stock Exchange.

The judge was not happy they had not left yet and were, in fact, arguing with him. "You told me yourself you cannot connect this woman with anything that has happened to those computers. When you can, come and see me."

Grady had asked for the names of any Marine Corps personnel who might have worked directly with Melissa and the only name Colonel Bartle could give him was that of Lieutenant Barnes, who happened to be deployed in Afghanistan. Colonel Bartle ordered Barnes to Bagram to engage in a teleconference with Grady Marcs and Special Agent Jimmy Steele.

It would take a full twenty-four hours to get him from frontline deployment back to Bagram because of military priorities. Grady asked the colonel to call the general and ask for an expedited airlift to Bagram. The colonel hesitated, but made the call. The general's secretary called back in fifteen minutes and said teleconference call with Lieutenant Barnes at Bagram Air base would be in five hours.

❧❧❧

Jimmy and Grady sat in a bar just off base and within sight of the telecommunications office where Lieutenant Barnes would appear on the ten-foot screen.

"I know we can tap her line, monitor her Internet traffic," Grady said.

"You don't want to do that. I know someone in the NSA who will do it for me and we won't have dirty fingers." Jimmy spent the next half hour on his cell phone and abruptly handed it to Grady.

The woman's voice on the other end was quiet, but she knew what she wanted from Grady. In half an hour she called Jimmy and he listened, frowning and shaking his head.

"Nothing. She isn't using her own computer at all. No traffic." He slid the phone into his jacket pocket. "The IP address in that log you have was used on a dynamic rotation of Internet users in San Francisco. The very moment the attack was made on the computer system in New York, a school teacher was using it to upload new grades." Jimmy looked at Grady. "I can send someone over there now and talk to her, convince her to show her computer to the agent, but that's not going to give us anything, is it?"

Grady shook his head. "It will just prove what we already know, this gal is sharp."

"What about the guy she was with when she first visited the server room? What's his story?"

"I didn't get much out of Brett, but it seems it was a well-connected family. He's in the hospital for at least another week, no-contact orders. That's worth following up on. It might just be a love interest she used, but then the guy might know something."

Jimmy shook his head. "If you promise to be nice, I can get the no-contact order lifted and we can talk to him. I just don't want the guy to die on us."

છખછ

Giving up the name of one of the wealthiest bankers on Wall Street was not something Brett did easily. He insisted on talking directly to an FBI agent and not over the phone with someone purporting to be an agent in San Diego. Jimmy respected that and had an agent in Brett's hospital room within half an hour.

Brett explained that giving up a family name could ultimately cost him his job and any hope of working on Wall Street again, but he understood the seriousness of the matter. Brett wrote the family name on a piece of paper and slid it across his desk to the agent. "That's his grandfather. The young man you want is Peter."

Grady raised his eyebrows when he heard the name. He laughed. Melissa was either very good in bed or she was somehow manipulating the grandson. No one from Melissa's class of people would have ever been allowed to associate with someone from that family. Grady was certain this was the connection he needed. Jimmy took another call from the quiet woman in the NSA. He listened for half an hour and smiled when he disconnected.

"She's a conspiracy nut job. Ten different conspiracy websites and she's on them most every night. Nut job insomniac. Do you get the connection with the family?"

Grady nodded his head, but did not get it completely. Why would the grandson of one of really the wealthiest banking family in the United States and perhaps even the world, work with a college dropout who was determined to prove the wealthy were surreptitiously trying to enslave the masses? "I know the theories well. I have been accused many times of willingly participating in parts of it when I was in Afghanistan. The 9/11 theory, well, I was part of that...you know." He winked. "This is odd. Any idea where this kid is?"

"He's been off the radar for years. We have an agent on his way over to the grandfather's office now. I will bet he is referred to a lawyer and will get nowhere. These people don't give up family members, period." Jimmy ordered another beer. "If we don't crack this in the next few hours, I need to turn it all over for a full-blown investigation, and it will get prioritized down, unless, of course, she does something stupid. The thinking internally will be to look for Arabs, not an MIT dropout, and we really have nothing on her. She has actually done the right thing for the NYSE, hasn't she? She gave good advice and they followed it and found a virus. Probably hers, but no one has any proof she is doing this, do you?"

Grady didn't like the way that was asked.

ༀༀༀ

The satellite connection was only fair and questions

and answers had to be repeated several times. Lieutenant
Barnes explained thoroughly his work with her in tracking down the marines who had been selling deployment
information through the computers on base. He almost
forgot the arrest at the daycare and recalled as much information as he could. Grady shook his head. He had
nothing. He thanked the Lieutenant and told him to stay
safe. The connection was cut and Grady walked out of
the office ahead of Jimmy. "I guess you have to turn it
over to the goons."

"They'll follow her around only because I tell them
to. Otherwise, nothing is going to be done really. I gave
my NSA contact your name and, when she has time,
she'll do some routine sniffing around and give you what
she has. I need to be back in Seattle in the morning."
Jimmy unlocked the rental car. "I'll drive you back to
your hotel and then I'm out of here."

Grady was silent until they approached the entrance
to the Holiday Inn. "I am going to pin this on her."

"Will I get a conviction?"

"That depends on how good you are."

಴ಌಌ

After the FBI special agent left his hospital room,
Brett answered his cell phone. Yes, he had the information about the two men who had tried a brute-force
attack. Yes, he had, subsequent to that attack, hired
Melissa based on a recommendation from his friend
Colonel Bartle. The men had been arrested and were out
on bail, awaiting trial. Yes, Melissa was instrumental in
gathering the evidence they now had. He gave Grady the
names and their contact information, the names and
phone numbers of their attorneys.

Jimmy was turning in his rental car when Grady

called him. "Melissa set up two guys to try a brute-force attack on the NYSE servers and then set herself up as a trusted consultant to track them down and she caught them at something she had engineered. This got her in the door. If I had nothing but time, I would be able to find her program on the NYSE servers and I could trace where she was working from, but we don't have time. What latitude do you have to call these attorneys and get these crackers to cooperate with me and trace their activity back to Melissa?"

Jimmy made the call and, before he walked on to the plane to Seattle, the first attorney called—a public defender. He would have his client in his office at nine the next morning. The second attorney called and agreed to meet at the public defender's office.

CHAPTER 36

Peter's grandfather rarely met with people. But he visited Brett in his hospital room, another lifting of the no-contact order. Brett spelled out how he thought Melissa had set up the ruse with the two hackers and then became the white knight and solved their problem but, in the meantime, had installed a script that ultimately affected Reed and Rowe. Just how that was done was being investigated by the FBI.

He explained how Melissa had deep connections with the military, a security clearance, and was a trusted consultant. None of this would stop the FBI from arresting her and charging her.

Peter's grandfather sighed. "I don't want the FBI arresting her. I don't want them involved. Can you imagine what happens to banking in this country if we ever let knowledge of this go public? She needs to end this and there is only one option. Thank you for your efforts in this, Mr. Douglass. I understand you are under some orders to take things easy and I want you to do just that. I will handle this from here. There is no more need to speak to the FBI."

❧❧❧

Peter's father listened without emotion. Peter was his only child now and what his own father was requiring him to do could ultimately cost him his life.

"Father, you are right that we need to something about this girl, but to have Peter do it. He's not capable of doing it."

"If one family fortune is affected, we are all affected. She has proven able to attack at will and where she is least expected to succeed. I have arranged to meet with Armand in Hamburg tomorrow. I want you to accompany me."

"Yes, Father."

❧❧❧

The flight to Hamburg was smooth and without incident. The two men were met at the airport and driven to the Schultz family home. Armand and his sons were waiting. Armand held out his right hand. "Peter Senior, so good to see you, but under such unfortunate circumstances. It is as if we have both lost our dear children."

"Armand, thank you for extending such good care and guidance to my grandson in Mexico. We have no need to shame our families. What you have chosen to do is correct. My grandson is at your disposal until you determine he has sufficiently paid a debt he owes to you."

The men slowly entered a large sitting room. Two waiters brought tea. There was no conversation for several minutes. Armand looked at his sons and then at Peter's father and grandfather. "Like I said, we have all lost here. I agree with you, Peter, when you told me you thought we should handle the affair of this woman amongst ourselves. It would be symbolic if your grandson, and your son, Peter, would take the responsibility to make the matter right and stop her permanently. Are you sure, Peter?"

"He facilitated the efforts, lied to all of us. Of course, in doing so, he stands the clear chance of being caught. If this is resolved successfully, as we think it needs to be, perhaps our young Peter will become useful again to both families. If not, well, then we'll see."

Armand sat quietly for a few minutes then nodded at one of the waiters. The waiter brought a phone and Armand called Father Gustavus.

ᕭᕲᕭᕲ

Father Gustavus explained to Peter he would probably only have to do this once and he would have repaid any debt he owed the Schultz family. It would be easy and quick. The young woman he had been associated with was becoming dangerous. She was threatening the stability of investor markets. They would visit her and entertain her for the night and Father Gustavus would provide further instructions. He expressed hope it would be a simple matter of convincing her to cease this senseless behavior, go back to her work as a security consultant, and no one would be the wiser. He knew what the Schultz family wanted, and it was very different from his expressed hope. There was no reason to alarm young Peter at this time. Father Gustavus had dressed in his black shirt with the little white square at the front of the collar.

On the way to dinner, they stopped at Melissa's house. She was in and nervous, at first, seeing a priest standing behind Peter. She listened to the plan to have dinner and talk about how to bring the events to an end, to wrap up what they were doing, and reconsider the merits of attacking the problem from a different angle.

"Peter, you disappeared. Where did you go? And

Klaus, what happened to him? What happened to your motorhome?"

"Melissa, let's talk about that at dinner. Join us, please." Father Gustavus was gracious in his tone and held his right hand out to touch hers. Melissa stepped back inside and shut the door. He looked over at Peter and smiled. "I am certain she will be with us in just a few minutes."

In fact, it was five minutes and she was carrying a purse. Father Gustavus knew five minutes meant she had called someone and, wherever they went, someone would be watching.

"I know this place here in Carlsbad, near Rancho. A bit expensive, but they have the best stuffed Portabella mushrooms." Melissa smiled at both of them. "Can you afford me?"

Father Gustavus nodded. When they arrived, he saw the three men from the parking lot. Three men all about the same age, in their mid-sixties, and obviously former military—the haircuts suggested they were still somehow involved in all things military. Amateur retirees. Melissa intentionally walked by them, without acknowledging them, and the Chinese man followed them with his eyes.

Father Gustavus talked eloquently of his language studies and showed off by translating the menu into Vietnamese out loud. He added vulgar expressions a Vietnamese might use to insult a Chinese national. The Chinese man with the wandering eyes was visibly shaken. Vietnam era military. Father Gustavus guessed the white man with his back to them was related to Melissa. The red haired man was a drinker and would be of little consequence.

"It's nice to see you have people who are interested in your wellbeing." Father Gustavus gulped his Manhattan. Melissa looked up with a false curiosity. Father Gustavus nodded his head toward the table with the three men. "Is that your father with his back to us? And those would be his war buddies. Vietnam. The Chinese fellow, when I was translating the menu into Vietnamese, it was a North Vietnamese dialect. I was insulting all of the mothers of China and he understood clearly what I was saying. He is so attentive even now."

Melissa sat back in her chair. "All right, who are you and what do you want from me?"

"Want? From you? I want nothing from you. But let me tell you what I know. I probably know more than you think." He accurately recounted the days she was in New York at Peter's family apartment and her visits to the server rooms in the bowels of the New York Stock Exchange. "I am not proficient with these new computer technologies, but I am educated in the practice of logical thinking. I do not gather evidence, rather I deduce. I come to the truth through reasoning. Now, I work for a family with a strong vested interest in increasing their family fortunes through investing. They see a direct correlation between your recent visits to New York and some...shall we say...unnerving incidents involving investor funds."

"You're a priest, and you work for a family? What kind of work do you do?"

Father Gustavus sensed a hint of sarcasm. "I take care of their spiritual needs." He ate one of the stuffed mushrooms in one bite. "Uhmm, yes, these are very good." He wiped his lips with the cloth napkin. "What kind of work do you do?"

"Peter here hasn't told you?"

"Actually not." Peter shook his head. "The subject never came up."

Melissa shrugged. "What I do is none of your business."

Father Gustavus breathed deeply and grunted as he exhaled. "But, my dear, it is my business now. As we speak, the family I work for has hired a team of German nationals who are skilled in the investigative arts. They are searching your house and you will never know they have been there, other than I am telling you now that they are there. Why are you attempting to interrupt the investment system? What would lead you to believe you would be at all effective and that you would not be caught?"

"I don't have to explain anything to you, ever. If you say you work for a family tied to the New York Stock Exchange, and you are a priest, then you are simply full of shit." She was still holding the fork she used to cut into her stuffed mushroom and she pointed it at Father Gustavus and then at Peter. "You two stay away from me. I should have figured you out a long time ago. You are both pigs and I will hurt you both." She stood abruptly, causing the three men at the table to stand as well. The four of them left the restaurant.

Father Gustavus sat back, smiling. "Too bad the catch of the day here isn't shark. The sharks in these waters are so well fed."

❧❧❧

Father Gustavus decided it was probably better if he completed this job himself. The three wise men were inconsequential to him, but Peter was not equipped to take care of them. They would probably hurt him and that would fuck things up, for sure.

He drove Peter to the lot where the motorhome had been stored after cleaning. "There is money in the refrigerator. A lot of it. You go get some gas, and drive this back to Mulege tonight."

'Is that what you brought me back to San Diego to do?"

"For now. I will be back in a couple of days and we can talk about how we finish this then."

The drunk was sitting in a car a block away from Melissa's house. The silent bullet to the back of his head made a mess, but Father Gustavus didn't see it. He never did. If you did your job right, you never had to look back. Simple logic. The Chinese man was hiding in the back yard and was actually surprised to see him. The gaping mouth of surprise was still there as he lay on his back, his throat slashed. The old man, the one with his back to him at the restaurant, looked out the kitchen window and then appeared on the back porch. He was not surprised. He looked resigned. Father Gustavus thought this was more fitting. The man was so full of sin, he expected this retribution from God and he took it silently. Father Gustavus next stood in the kitchen listening to Melissa call for her father. She walked briskly into the kitchen and before she saw him, she was unconscious.

The decapitation on the side of the highway north of Ensenada was necessary. It would all be reported as part of the unholy war on drugs in Baja California, and no one would ever know it was really a part of the holy war for control of the resources God intended his chosen few to have. The charter boat was waiting for him. It was necessary to warm up the engine, but soon they motored into the dark. "Nothing for the sharks tonight. Such a pity, Enrique."

"*Sí*, such a pity."

CHAPTER 37

Grady dialed into the public defender's office at fifteen minutes to nine and both young men were present. Yes, they could start. One of them had saved all conversations with the person he met on line known as "satanwithinyou." The code attached to the chats was Melissa's "Banker's Delight," slightly modified for an external brute-force attempt.

"Well, I'm not the prosecutor or your attorney and I have no idea how you are going to get out of this, but I can assure you what you had was very dangerous and what you did, in my mind, was explicitly illegal," Grady said. "However, this helps me connect this woman to the stock exchange servers. I know she was setting you up in order to get inside. Hope you guys straighten up but, if I ever catch you in my computer, I'll kill you."

The young men laughed. Grady did not.

The call from Jimmy was unexpected. Grady was going to call him with the evidence and hopefully watch an arrest. "Turn your TV on. CNN."

Grady looked at a police investigation alongside a highway and the banner under the screen shot indicated it was an investigation into the beheading of an American woman working with the United States Marine Corps in San Diego.

"Jesus Christ. What's the word in your world?"

"It's bigger than this. Her father, who also contracted to the Marine Corps, as you know, and his two business associates were executed, not killed, executed. Whoever did this is very good." Jimmy breathed deeply. "This is going to get played two ways in the press. They'll try to call it a drug war execution, but pretty quickly it is going to be discovered the old men didn't do anything with drugs, at least as far as I know. Nor did the girl. Did the boys give you anything?"

"A bit. She was pretty deep into the New World Order conspiracy stuff. I can see a crude connection between those whacko theories and using her technical skills to interrupt the stock exchange. But this. She really pissed someone off."

"Was it you?"

"Sometimes I wish, but I got her on her playing field, It's just too bad I didn't get to see her get arrested."

"The other play is going to be retribution against the United States government for helping the Mexican government with those drug lords. That's the one people are going to believe."

"Doesn't sound like you believe either of them."

"Nope, I have two theories. One, you got drunk on tequila, did them all in, and can't remember anything. And two, it's connected to the stock exchange threat and we will never know who ordered the hit. But it was professional. And considering these are nobodies, the press will drop it, our director will hardly notice it happened, and that will be the end."

"You sound bitter."

"And you're not?"

"Not at all. I got her. That's all that matters to me." Grady turned the TV off. "The only thing that would have made this all better is if someone over at Northwest Bank, with a set of balls and brains, had gone after this thing before she got brave. Is there anything else you want from me?"

Jimmy was silent for a moment. "Get your butt back up here to Seattle. It's going to be seventy degrees, sunny as hell and I want to get drunk on bad beer on your new deck."

❦

The free people who wandered the concourse, waiting for their flights, rarely thought about this freedom they enjoyed. Grady had known this his entire life and it always bothered him. He thought about Mark Burgess and dialed his number.

"San Diego? You get your ass out of there unless you're carrying that Glock."

"Don't worry. I'm fine."

"Fucking bastards going after civilian contractors. I have half a mind to re-up, march on Mexico City, and clean that crap up."

"Yes, you do have half a mind and you're too old. Instead of a uniform, they would be fitting you with Depends." Mark laughed so hard he could not respond. "I really called because I actually care about you. How's Derrick doing?" Grady asked.

"He's fine. We've talked a lot, set some parameters, and I even went to a therapy session with him. I know the lady hates me, but what the hell. The Taliban hates me and I fear them. She can bugger off. I'm sure he's gay and he's exploring around. It's all new and exciting to him. He thinks I hate him, in spite of the fact I keep telling him that no matter what he ends up being, I will love him, but that lady therapist keeps telling him guys like me hate gay guys and so he's got some work to do."

"Well, good. Just killing time and wanted to connect."

"Yeah, thanks. Hey, that nut job who interviewed me called back and wants to present new evidence to me in another interview. You want to join me?"

Grady laughed and almost said no. "Maybe. Call me in a couple of days and ask me again."

He looked at his watch. His flight boarded in an hour. He dialed Grady Junior's cell phone. "Hey, I'm flying in about three hours from now. You know that case of beer I have sitting in the cabinet in the basement?...Yeah, the real crappy stuff that's been sitting there for like two years. Get that into the fridge in the basement for me. If Jimmy Steele gets there before I do, give him one of those, not my good stuff upstairs."

CHAPTER 38

*K*yrie...eleison...Christe, eleison...Kyrie...eleison
...
Father Gustavus beat his chest hard three times.
The hollow cavity of his chest let out a hard noise that
filled the candle-lit storage room he had converted into
his private chapel. He quietly mumbled the readings and
reflected on them and then hastily prepared the chalice
with wine and the small piece of bread.

"*Sanctus, Sanctus, Sanctus Dominus Deus Sabaoth.
Pleni sunt caeli et terra gloria tua. Hosanna in excelsis.
Benedictus qui venit in nomine Domini. Hosanna in ex-
celsis.*"

Peter sat in the corner of the room, observing. He
had been to the celebration of the Catholic Mass many
times in his life and had come to appreciate the ritual,
even if he understood nothing about it. It was all silent
motion now.

No one was there to ring a bell when the bread and
the chalice of wine were lifted.

"*Agnus Dei, qui tollis peccata mundi: miserere
nobis. Agnus Dei, qui tollis peccata mundi: miserere*

nobis. Agnus Dei, qui tollis peccata mundi: dona nobis pacem."

Father Gustavus stood with his head held low into his chest, silent for several minutes. *Ecce Agnus Dei, ecce qui tollit peccata mundi. Beati qui ad cenam Agni vocati sunt. Domine, non sum dingus ut intres sub tectum meum: sed tantum dic verbo, et sanabitur anima mea.*

Real tears streamed from his eyes and then he wept openly, gasping for breath as he shuddered in emotional agony. "I am so sorry. I am so sorry. I am such an unworthy servant. Corpus Christi. Amen."

Father Gustavus sat on the small wooden stool for several minutes and then stood, facing the ornate crucifix on the chapel wall, held his arms outstretched. "The Mass is ended, go in peace. Thanks be to God."

The chalice and silver plate were cleaned and the candles quickly extinguished. Father Gustavus placed his vestments carefully on the makeshift altar and turned to Peter. "Good to see you made it to mass finally. I am in here every morning at six sharp, when I do not celebrate the Eucharist in the town church. You would benefit from attending more frequently."

෬෬෬

Peter had never been able to eat breakfast. He could drink coffee and even a little orange juice, but the thought of hard, greasy food in his stomach before noon made him cringe.

Father Gustavus liked what he called the five-bacon breakfast. Five slices of bacon, four sausages, three eggs over easy, two slices of toast, and one glass of orange juice. "If you wake up at all, you should celebrate the morning and eat well because by nightfall, you may be in dire circumstances and have no access to food. Pity the warrior who has eaten no breakfast, who finds himself in peril by happy hour, and has no provisions. You certainly will not survive that night."

Martin brought more coffee. "The police were here again yesterday afternoon and I invited them in. I welcomed them to look around and they did. Mrs. Gustavus came by and they spoke to her briefly and thanked her. I offered to fix them something to eat, but they declined. I have filled the freezer with meat and actually opened it while they were here so they could see inside of it."

"Thank you, Martin."

Peter sat back reflectively. "He is so good. Wherever did you find household help like him?"

Father Gustavus seemed to ignore Peter as he sopped up egg yolk with his last piece of toast. He chewed carefully for several minutes and looked up. "He is also in debt to the Schultz family."

"Did he steal something?"

Father Gustavus shook his head and sighed. "You are like a pathetic little gossip. You need to know all these little personal details about people. If I tell you he owes a debt to the Schultz family, that is all you need to know. Is that clear?"

He slammed his hand on the table sending cups and plates scattering to the dining room floor. Martin appeared quickly and swept them up.

Father Gustavus sat forward in his chair. "Now you listen to me. I took care of the San Diego thing because I knew you would get hurt. You are the most useless example of a human being I have ever seen. You are good at the kill, but you have nothing else and, right now, you are of no use to this family. If I had my way right now I would cut your balls off, shove them down your mouth, and, while you were still alive, cut pieces of you off and feed them to the sharks. I hate little crap shits like you."

He sat back in his chair, smiling. "The family wants me to train you. From what I told them, and I am sorry I told them anything, you will be useful, but only if I train you. I said to them it is impossible to train the children of the wealthy. If they have transgressed against the family, they should be fed to the sharks, but, no, they feel so sorry for you that you lost your childhood friend at the grove, that you saw him murdered that night. You have the kill in you and they want you alive. They want you to be useful. I doubt that can ever happen, but I work for them and today your training begins." Father Gustavus sipped loudly from the wine. "I know you can kill, I just need to teach you how. Right after you are done eating, I am going to begin teaching you."

❧❧

Father Gustavus unlocked the gun cabinet. Peter was a natural. His eyes glistened and his mouth was slightly opened as if to say something, but he was overwhelmed.

"Do you like to shoot?" Father Gustavus asked.

"I've only shot with a shot gun and a rifle on my grandfather's hunting ranch in Montana."

"You've killed deer and such."

"Oh, yes." There was lust in Peter's voice, as if they were talking about sex.

Father Gustavus knew, for young Peter, this was better than sex. "Excellent. Well, I'll bet you have not fired many of these."

"No. They look pretty nice though."

"They are very nice. Let's begin by learning how to disassemble them, clean them, and properly reassemble them. Please note the order they are in. Never put them back out of order. Never."

CHAPTER 39

Jimmy left at ten and called Grady at ten twenty. "Something just came in and I need you back in San Diego tomorrow morning. Go see General Durning as soon as you get there. Ticket is waiting for you and your flight leaves at five-fifteen. I am going to walk over and give you copies of this. Have you ever gone up against the Mossad?"

Grady smiled. "Overrated pussies."

芝芝芝

General Durning was in fatigues, two bright stars pinned to both lapels. His black beret fitted perfectly. "I'm glad Special Agent Steele sent you back. Do you know anything about the fellow Melissa was working with?"

Grady shook his head and sighed. "I was trying to gather cyber evidence and wasn't focused on any accomplices. What she was doing, she was doing alone. I know she gained access."

"We picked up some German nationals, trying to dispose of three bodies. Melissa's father was one of them. They didn't seem to realize, or even care, that they were on military land. The MPs took them in for trespassing and then found the bodies in their car. I got called in because of what these three were doing for me in recovering stolen weapons."

"Yes, we spoke of this before. Who were the German nationals?"

"All they said was they are employed by a family in Germany to tend to their personal business, to handle things. I talked to one of them late last night and my German is still very good. He didn't want to talk much, but we showed him aerial pictures of Guantanamo and his tongue loosed up a bit. I really don't ordinarily participate in these interrogations, but they were my men and now it's personal.

"They aren't currently active duty military and NCIS is only looking into the fact the dead bodies were found on their land and the fact that some foreign nationals are in the country without passports. Low priority, considering two marine captains were killed on base last night by their own men." General Durning leaned forward. "I have them for the next twenty-four hours because NCIS likes me so much and just wants them deported and out of their hair. I want you to talk to them."

"You have an excellent army intelligence unit here. I think they are better suited—"

"Politics. I send them in to ask questions and the brass all the way up to the joint chiefs is wondering why army spies are working on NCIS gigs. Division of labor. I just want to know who they are working for and why my guys were killed."

❧❧❧

The older of the four, Herbst Breck, was the only one with any military training. The others were police academy rejects. Breck ended up in the BND, German intelligence, and was closely involved with the Israeli Mossad in tracking old Nazis in South America, until he tipped off three of them, allowing them to escape capture. After serving fifteen years in the BND, his less-than-stellar military career was over. He was not tried for giving away national secrets—they were Israeli national secrets. He found a few of the brass above him willing to look the other way if he would just disappear. He found work as a private investigator, willing to take on the dirty jobs, even what American consumers of espionage movies know as "wet work."

He could kill and he could clean. He had worked closely in the BND with a man who now called himself Father Enrique Gustavus. It was Gustavus who had given him the locations of the old Nazis and suggested they would be useful on a project he had. Breck explained he understood this was why the Israelis never came after him, either. He got the intelligence from them, even though it seemed to hurt their efforts. The old Nazis ended up dead, anyway, after executing one of their own—the Gustavus Project—setting off a vendetta from some other old Nazis the Israelis could not find. That was until they came out of hiding to execute the vendetta. Gustavus killed all of them, in the end, and getting five ultra-secret Nazis along with the ones Breck tipped off was seen as excessive. He retired from the Mossad shortly after photographs of him were given to the Israeli Prime Minister. He never knew what was in the pictures, but his retirement was permanent.

Gustavus took employment with a family in Hamburg. His office door simply said "Special Projects" and it was well known that he usually lived in Mexico.

General Durning knew the answer to his question before his asked. "And why did he give up Gustavus?"

"Breck wants Gustavus's job."

"Wants us to do the dirty work. Figures. What is Gustavus to us? Is he useful?"

"Could be. I haven't been around that kind of work for a while, so I don't know what kind of things you guys are up to."

General Durning laughed. "We have the world's largest private army ostensibly on protective duty for citizens and the State Department in Iraq and you don't know how we could use a guy like Gustavus?" He lit a cigar. "Would you be interested in talking to him, maybe get him back here to talk to me?"

"Spy versus spy work usually does not end well, and I like cybercrime. I have a nice family."

"Yeah, I know the feeling. Let me propose something to you. You just get him here, and I will be his minder. I need him to stop some guys who are pretty close to stealing some technology we've been developing for twenty years. I'll deposit three hundred thousand dollars in your account today if you agree to drive down and talk to him. Take a copy of the tape we made of Breck. Breck rolled on him, wants his job, you're doing him a favor, and I get a job done as well as keeping tabs on the guy who killed my posse." Durning sucked hard on the cigar and blew the smoke. "Breck won't last two days."

"Like I said, I like cybercrime. Bits and bytes don't kill you. And for me, this whole matter is closed." Grady stood and moved toward the door to leave. He stopped, his back to the general. "What's the technology and who's stealing it?"

Durning smiled. He liked patriots. "I'll tell you a bit, just up to the point where I might give away state secrets and get shot for treason. Let me start by saying it's not the Muslims, and it involves the only standing great example of the failure of communism."

Grady listened patiently, nodding, taking only mental notes. He knew very well this was more serious than the petty intrigue Gustavus was involved in.

"Those three guys Gustavus took out had just given me two names. I knew they were protecting his daughter and I did not share that. Maybe I should have, but it's too late now. We didn't—and still don't—know why Gustavus assassinated them. He had his reasons. What I do know is the defense and security of this country, and I need someone who owes me to finish this thing. I will handle him after that. Get him up here to talk to me and you're out of this."

Grady left the general's office silently. It was time to serve again.

స్రోస్రో

Jimmy had already spoken with General Durning and sent copies of some of the information the FBI had on Father Enrique Gustavus. There was a lot of high-level interest in returning him to the United States, but FBI resources were not going to visit him in Mexico and extradite him back. The murders of the three United States Army Intelligence civilian operatives in San Diego would be kept silent, for now. It was not in anyone's interest to reveal sensitive military weapons were being stolen and only partially recovered. Gustavus did not assassinate them for their intelligence work. They were in his way on another matter. The interest the FBI had in him could easily disappear. Jimmy told Grady to offer him a deal. They would be interested in knowing if he was involved in the murder of Melissa Eggers within Mexico—a Mexican matter but still of serious interest to the FBI. The fact that she was the daughter of one of the civilian operatives was a concern and perhaps might point to other activities that were crucial to national security.

Grady smiled. He knew well the system of tradeoffs and mirrors, all carefully designed to distract the civilian population while political agendas were quietly carried out.

CHAPTER 40

Mark Burgess was sitting on the curb at Lindbergh Field as several cars jockeyed to get close to pick up or drop off passengers. He could see Grady's rental as it turned the corner. He stood, walked in front of moving cars, waved him down, opened the passenger door, tossed his bag into the back of the SUV, and climbed into the passenger seat as Grady continued to roll.

"I'd like to see these little bitches in a war zone. These people are idiots."

"Most people are." Grady shook his hand. "Glad you could make it."

"So, what's this about some fat bastard priest in Mexico? And what the hell does this have to do with some chick stealing money from a little bank in Seattle? Then she ends up with her head cut off. And now you're talking about cutting down someone in China who is about to steal our next great secret weapon. What the hell are you getting me into?" The voice was loud and harsh, but the smile on Colonel Burgess's face told Grady everything. He was going to enjoy it, like he always did.

෴

They drove slowly through the streets of Tijuana. Mark eyed every person who approached the SUV, wondering if any of them wanted to kidnap him, or maybe try. He thought it would be fun. Grady shook his head. "I'm glad I was never one of your bad guys."

"Oh, I'm not that evil. I just like my entertainment a little rough." Mark waved at a small group of men staring at him. "What do you think we're worth down here? A million? Two million?"

"Let's see, you get a lousy army pension. You have a half-written book and you don't have a marketable personality. I'd say, after they found all this out, they would let you go and find someone else."

Mark snorted out of his nose. "By the way, how much are you paying me for this?"

"Half."

"Of what?"

"Three hundred thousand. Half of it was dropped in my account today, the other half when this priest shows up at Durning's door. So one fifty for you minus the taxes I owe on your portion."

"Really. Three hundred thousand dollars. Is your mercenary money always this good?"

"Nope. Demand drives the price." Grady smiled. "You know this guy was Mossad."

"Yeah, you told me. When I was a captain, I got sent out to Beirut and tangled with three of them. After I killed the first one, they left me alone. They have a big reputation but like every branch of service anywhere, the reputation is always bigger than the person. They hide behind the reputation. If you believe the reputation and, for even one second, think they could be better than you, you've dug your own grave."

"Yes, you've mentioned that to me about nine thousand times."

"And you live, making three hundred thousand dollars on a cake walk."

"And I live."

℘℘

Mulege in September was tolerably hot. Even the humidity was bearable. The snow birds start to return, depending on what part of El Norte they summered in. The town started to recapture the lively, festive feel the winter residents loved so much.

No one anymore assumed any town was immune from resident evil.

Crimes occurred in every country, and Mulege, Mexico was no exception, but the festive life went on and people tried to live out decent, happy lives, avoiding the evil and trying to embrace the good.

Mark walked up to a street vendor selling ornate handled knives. In decent Spanish, he negotiated the price down a bit, knowing he could have gone further, then paid with American dollars. The vendor gave him a hand-tooled leather sheath. "Needs sharpening, but nothing like a backup knife."

The drive up to the house was slow and cautious. Grady drove by once, then doubled back on a different road, stopping directly in front. "Cameras. Three in front."

Mark nodded.

The two casually dressed Caucasian men walked slowly to the front door and Martin opened it before they could ring the bell. "Welcome to Mulege, How can I be of service?"

"We would like to speak to Father Antonio Gustavus, please." Grady stood with his hands clasped behind his back. He always had his primary knife tucked into his belt there and reached easily by either the right or left hand.

"One moment, please."

Grady pointed to the cameras in the foyer.

"Martin, shame on you." The booming voice echoed in the foyer. "Let my guests in, please. Gentlemen, Father Antonio Gustavus." He held out a massive hand. "I have been expecting you."

Mark laughed through his nose. "No you haven't. You have no idea who we are or why we are here. I worked with you guys. I know what you are doing."

"Worked with us guys?" Father Gustavus stepped back, his arms spread wide.

"Beirut. Nineteen-eighty-one. You want his name, rank, and serial number?" Mark stepped forward. "I kept his dog tags. You want them back? Maybe his children would enjoy having them."

The gregarious Father Gustavus became quiet. He looked silently at one then the other and nodded his head. "I am honored they sent two of you. Let's go in there and sit down. Martin, please bring these gentlemen some iced tea." He led the way then stopped. "Please do not worry, I will sip from your glasses first if you suspect I may have told Martin to poison your tea."

✌✍✌

Father Gustavus listened quietly to the proposition. "You are here just to get me to visit General Durning. Is that all?"

Grady shrugged. "And I get paid more if you do."

"Excellent."

"The FBI is aware of your talents, and also aware

that, in your line of work, the three gentlemen you encountered at the home belonging to Melissa Eggers were there to interrupt your work. They are also interested in the death of Melissa Eggers, albeit on Mexican soil. They are more interested, however, in the security of the United States of America."

"I see." Father Gustavus placed his hands in front of him as if in prayer. "The work I was doing was basic cleanup of a messy situation. I work for a family, a German family."

"Yes, we know, Breck told us. I have a recording if you want to hear it from him."

"Breck." Father Gustavus was not smiling. "I never liked him. Did you know he belongs to one of these wild new-age cults? They run around in G-strings, screaming their fool heads off, and they call that worship. They're a bunch of hedonistic sex addicts, that's all." He tapped his fingers together. "Breck"

Martin appeared with the tea. He served each glass separately on a round coaster then picked up the tray, gave a short bow, and left. Mark picked up his glass and took a long, noisy drink, smiling as he set it back on the small table.

"So, Mr. Marcs, who is it you believe I work for?"

"It's none of my business."

"One might say, if I entertain the offer you are presenting on behalf of General Durning, that I would be serving two masters, and that just does not work. Jesus our Lord Himself tells us that. 'No servant can serve two masters. Either he will hate the one and love the other, or he will be devoted to the one and despise the other. You cannot serve both God and Money.' That's from Luke. We find the same quote in Mathew. I serve God, therefore I cannot serve money."

"You serve God? From what I can tell, you serve the

financial interests of one wealthy family, and their sole desire is to acquire more wealth."

"Mr. Marcs, you are obviously suffering from a devastating lack of faith and exposure to correct theology." Father Gustavus sipped his tea. "Please understand if I accepted General Durning's offer to work on behalf of the United States of America, I would not find this to be a conflict between my devotion to God and the temptation to serve money as my master. Indeed, not at all. If General Durning likes whatever work I do for him and compensates me, then I am merely taking care of my own talents, adding to my own care and the care of those who depend on me. I see no conflict at all. All I said was, one might think I was serving two masters when, in fact, my employer and General Durning are one and the same master, deigned by God to be obeyed and loved."

"Oh, here it comes, Grady. A theological dissertation on how God has chosen a few elite people to govern this great world for Him. You know what this is, don't you?"

Grady smiled. "Yes, I do. He sees no conflict with killing for a family he considers the true rulers of the world and a country he thinks is owned and governed by this and a few other families." Grady stood. "I doubt it would work out for you. Let me talk with General Durning, tell him what we discovered here in Mulege, and I'll have the general call you."

Father Gustavus stood. "Please tell General Durning I would be honored to be considered for this most worthy assignment. Please have him call me at his earliest convenience." Father Gustavus handed both men his card. "Let me show you to the door."

Grady and Mark walked ahead of Father Gustavus into the foyer. Mark heard the click of the Glock behind him and pulled his knife before the gun could be aimed, slicing through the silk shirt into the priest's heart. Grady pulled his knife and lunged at Father Gustavus as he turned with a head-high round kick, catching Grady on the side of the head but not able to knock him down. Mark pulled the second knife, the ornate-handled one bought on the streets of Mulege, and threw it, striking Father Gustavus in the side of his neck. Grady lunged again at the staggering priest, pushing his knife deep into his belly and slicing upward, quickly stepping away from the flowing blood and entrails. He instinctively pulled his second knife from the strap on his leg and stood silently over the dead priest.

"He got fat and slow."

"Yes he did." Grady followed the cable from one of the cameras with his eyes, noticed where it entered the wall. He kicked open the door of a small storage room and ripped the recording device from the wall. They walked slowly to the rented SUV. "Why was he going to kill us?"

"No clue."

CHAPTER 41

Peter noticed the front door slightly ajar. He pushed it open slowly and stepped softly through the foyer.

This was not normal. The door was never left open. Martin was standing over the body of the dead priest. Peter quietly approached. "Now what do we do?"

Martin smiled. "Let's get out of here. There's cash in his office, lots of it, and the bitch wife is gone for a few days."

"They'll think we did this."

"No, two guys came, Americans. And there are video cameras everywhere. The police will find the cameras and see what really happened."

"Where is the tape these cameras feed?"

"In there." Martin pushed the door to the storage room open and sighed. "Shit. Well, no matter, I need to get out of here. When they know he's dead, they will come after us. Trust me."

"Who?"

"My family. Your family. What does it matter? You're in more danger than I am. I'm just deviant, you killed two of them. And you tried to ruin them financially. They are so going to slice you to pieces."

"I didn't have anything to do with the money. That was all her and she's gone." Peter walked around the house, pacing from room to room, scratching his head. "Yeah, let's get out of here. I don't have a passport, so how do I get back into the states?"

"We drive to TJ and there is someone Father Gustavus knew who does favors. He can arrange a passport." Martin went to the priest's office and opened the large safe in the floor. He pulled out two bags of US dollars and a bag of Mexican Pesos. "I counted out about seventy grand in each of the bags once, a little more in Pesos which are useless after we get to the border. Once we're in the states, you have access to cash, right?"

"When does the wife come back?"

"Two, three days. We need to be in the states when she gets here. We'll have to ditch the Mercedes. We'll do that in TJ, maybe just give it to the passport guy. You have another vehicle up that way?"

"Several, any kind you want."

Martin gassing the Mercedes was a normal sight. Everyone just waved. He signed the bill for the gas and they drove North. Martin removed the Russian language bible from the CD player and threw it out the window. Neither of them spoke for the first two hours. They stopped at a gas station to fill up so they could use the restrooms. Peter was waiting in the Mercedes when Martin returned.

"You drive for a while."

Peter got into the driver's seat and started the engine. "What did you do to the family?"

Martin raised his eyebrows and was silent. He smiled and laughed lightly. "I was a bad boy."

"Not as bad as me, I suspect."

"By the way, are you going to slice my throat?"

"No. I thought about that, but I actually like you. You were so helpful with that college kid."

"Yeah, poor guy. But, hey. You know?" Martin looked out the window and was silent for a while. "You've met the Schultz family, I take it."

"My grandfather has known them since he was a boy, and one of my great aunts married one of them before the war, so they are cousins, pretty distant, but still we're all related."

"Yeah it's like that with those families."

"You're not related."

"I was taken in as an orphan. Not sure why. They are so into their own bloodline—purity, and all that. I was just an orphan from southern Germany and I was never going to be tall and blond. All my family were short, dark-haired mountain people and my parents were killed. I asked about all that once and I think they suggested one of the Schultz family members somehow killed my parents.

"Your English is pretty good."

"They sent me to one of their families in New York for high school and then college."

"Sounds like they liked you. Why were you working for the priest?"

"I seduced the cousin I was living with, the father. I was fourteen then and didn't say anything about it until I was eighteen. The guy went to prison and it ruined him. The Schultz family had to disown him. I knew it would ruin him, too, and, when I was done with college, I admitted I planned it all along. I could have gone to prison myself for lying to a court when I was an adult—perjury, you know—so they moved me to Mexico when Father Gustavus was moved there."

"What did he ever do to be sent into exile?"

"He wasn't. He chose Mulege when the family offered to move him. He was useful."

"I think I know what he did to Melissa—"

"You have no idea what he was capable of doing. One of his favorite things was to feed the corpses to the sharks."

"Is that all he did for the family, kill?"

"Pretty much. If the truth were ever told, I would guess two hundred, maybe more."

"They had a lot of enemies."

"Have. For what I did to the family, I was the houseboy until I turned thirty, and there was no guarantee I would have been allowed to live. Five more years of helping him move bodies, clean up, lie, cover for him. No thanks. I don't know who those guys were that killed him, or why he wanted to kill them first, but I am free, thanks to them."

ఆఇఆ

The Mercedes rolled quietly through one of the better neighborhoods of Tijuana at one-thirty in the morning. High up on the hill, overlooking the teeming northern Mexican city, all one could see were the lights and not the angry poverty coursing through the streets and alleys. Martin parked the car in the driveway of a large, unfinished home. They sat in the car until a short, fat man emerged from the side of the house and motioned for them. They walked along the side, past a small pool in the back yard, to a stucco-covered shed. Inside two other men sat around a small table, smoking and drinking beer.

The man who'd met them in the driveway looked first at Martin, sorted through several passports, pulled one out and handed it to him. "You are now Sean Danby, resident of Houston, Texas." He handed the passport to

Martin. The picture of the younger, dark-haired man was close, very close. Martin nodded. The man stared at Peter and shook his head. "You will be difficult. I do not get a lot of tall guys, and your hair. Can you shave your head?"

Peter shrugged. "Sure. Hair grows back."

"Let's do that now." The man spoke some quiet Spanish to one of the other men. He motioned for Peter to sit and plugged in electric hair shears. In a few minutes, Peter's hair was piled on the floor. The man looked again and nodded. "Now you look like one of the former marines who come down here, get drunk, and lose their passport." He threw one at Peter and the generic Caucasian face with a shaved head was a good match. "You are now Jeffery Wilcox. Resident of San Diego, California."

"What if they have applied for replacement passports?"

"They haven't. It costs me money to get that information, and I know, for a fact, these have not been reported lost or stolen. I will need twenty thousand dollars for each of them. The guys who lose their passports down here—it's usually in a whore house or buying drugs and it takes them a long time to figure out what to do. Not very smart guys." He pointed at his head.

"We can't take the Mercedes into the states," Martin said.

"How old is it?"

"A year, brand new then." Martin put the key on the table. "We can find a car in the states and we just need to walk through customs."

"Thirty thousand for the passports and I will clean and sell the Mercedes."

"And the cash. I can't use the pesos. There's fifty thousand in pesos. I have over one hundred thousand dollars I want to get to the other side."

The three men spoke in Spanish for several minutes.

The first man nodded. "We will take the pesos and Armando here will be waiting for you on the other side. You will see a Seven Eleven store and he will be parked in the lot across the street. He will see you and flash his lights. He can give you a ride into San Diego if you like."

※※※

By two-forty-five, Peter and Martin, having drunk down several beers and tequila shots, stood in line to walk back into the United States. People ahead of them looked back, the odor of liquor intentionally strong. Martin went first and it was a thirty-second formality. He was just visiting his friend Jeffrey, pointing back at Peter, and was flying back to Houston tomorrow. The agent handed the passport back and motioned for Peter. Same formality, but this time the agent spoke. "You're not driving, are you? Take a taxi or something. You guys stink."

"We have a ride waiting, up by the Seven Eleven."

"All right. Welcome back to the States."

※※※

They thanked Armando, tipped him several hundred dollars, and motioned for a taxi. Peter told him to drive to the W Hotel in downtown San Diego.

At the front desk, Peter asked to use the phone. It would be almost seven in the morning in New York. He spoke several different unrelated words into the phone and then a string of numbers. "I am at the W Hotel in San Diego. I need verification of credit for the hotel and my credentials sent here."

The woman's voice confirmed his identity and asked to speak to the clerk. The clerk wrote down some numbers and hung up. "Very good. We will put you into a suite, two bedrooms, a small kitchen, separate baths. Can I have something from the kitchen sent up?" He slid two key cards across the counter. "Welcome to the W."

"Please. A couple of steaks, salads, some red wine. Does that sound good to you, Martin?"

Martin nodded.

"Let's go up. I need a shower."

"Now your family knows you are here."

"Of course, they do. They are not the ones who are mad at me. Well, maybe a little."

After enjoying a drink from the bar and the view from the balcony, Martin sat on the large couch. "Now what?"

Peter dried off from his shower. "What do you mean?"

"You. Where do you go? And what can I do?"

"I am going back home to be with my father and my grandfather and live the life they expect me to live. I will do so until we are certain I am in no legal danger. As for the Schultzes, my grandfather will do everything he can to protect me. You? I don't know. What will you do?"

"I don't know what the statute of limitations is for perjury, but I'll bet there is one. I don't know how forgiving the family would be." Martin finished his drink. "I have my split of the hundred grand—"

Peter waved his hand. "I don't need that money. When I wake up in the morning, I'll have access to more money than you can ever imagine. That's yours."

"Really? Thanks." Martin sat back on the couch.

"Look, I really do like you. I can buy a motorhome here in San Diego and, when I find it in the next day or so, I want you to drive it to New York. I will need to fly out of here in the next two days or so, meet with my grandfather and my father, keep a low profile while they smooth things over with the Schultz family. Legally, I'm on meds for something really rare and I can get off on that. But I cannot go back to my friends and cousins for a while. You get my motorhome back there and then hang with me and we'll look into your perjury thing. Partners in crime. Who knows what we can think of doing? Hell, I helped almost take out the computers in the New York Stock exchange."

"You think we're pretty safe then, huh? For now?"

"Until we get in trouble again."

Martin answered the knock to let the room service in.

CHAPTER 42

Jimmy Steele said he could smell rain. "You didn't get out in time."

"No real offers on the house. I got the Jackson Hole cabin sold. Didn't make any money on it."

"Yeah, but you're rich. You should give me, a humble civil servant, a few hundred thousand so I could buy a Jackson Hole cabin."

"That wouldn't buy you a shack there." Grady stood to stretch. "You want another beer?" Jimmy nodded and Grady returned in a minute with two cold ones.

"I filed the report with the information you gave me," Jimmy said. "The NYSE completely revamped their security. Northwest Bank denies they have any evidence of a crime, and I will pursue that for a while if they use federal money to replace the stolen money. My guess is they will sell off some stock to cover the losses and never have to talk with us about the matter again. If I catch them, Charles and your buddy Sam will go to prison. My bet is they are going to play it close to the chest as long as they can and just eat the losses in accounting tricks."

"You know I have no dog in that fight. I was straight

up with you and will have no contact with them again. Clean fingernails."

"Hey, haven't got that Chinese national yet."

"Did he steel the transmogriphyer?"

"The what?"

"The silly secret weapon."

"Hell, I don't know. We never share intelligence." Jimmy drank from the beer. "I got something brewing. I may need to talk to you."

"Cell phone number doesn't change. What's up?"

"What do you know of the ELF?"

"Earth Liberation Front. Granola-sucking spoiled rich kids burning other people's houses down."

"You hold that thought. By the way, before I forget, I need to borrow your mower."

Grady waved. "So, this ELF case?"

"You know anything about the North American Electrical Reliability Council?"

"More than I want to."

"Good. Excellent, in fact." Jimmy sat back in the deck chair. "In your report you said the priest drew on you guys first. From behind."

"Yes, I was ahead of Mark and he heard—"

"Claimed he heard. Alleged."

Grady nodded, sticking his lower lip out. "Claimed he heard the safety on a Glock. Alleged." He smiled at Jimmy. "It was a Glock, right? The gun they found on the priest?"

"Yes, I most certainly think it was. Traced it back to some French colonial and then everything got real quiet about that Glock."

" And now it is all quiet, right?"

"All quiet."

"You going after that kid, Peter?"

"Who?"

"The co-conspirator."

"Oh yeah. I wanted to forget. You see some things just resolve themselves if you let them. Seems customs agents found a motorhome out in the desert just this side of the Mexican border. Inside was this kid, Peter, and one dead body. Outside there was a big hole and it seemed to the agents Peter was about to bury the body." Jimmy got up and started walking down the steps to the yard. He paused. "You wouldn't know anything about that, would you?"

Grady looked at him without expression.

"Didn't think so. Problem is this guy Peter has very big money behind him and is some sort of certified psycho. They're almost finished with the evals. Then they decide if there are any charges. He's free until further notice. Nice to have a rich daddy, no?"

About the Author

Shawn Rohrbach earned his BA in Medieval Philosophy at the Seminary of Christ the King in British Columbia, Canada, and his MFA in Writing at Naropa University in Boulder, Colorado. Rohrbach is the author of nine books, having won the 2008 Indie Book Award for Sports and Fitness. He lives and writes in San Diego, California, and travels frequently through the Southwest and Mexico to inform his stories and sample the tequila.